MAKE IT LAST
A COMPLETE ROMANCE NOVEL

A Novel By,
CHRISTINE GRAY

D1529097

Your FACE would

Look better BETWEEN our pages!

Check us out at www.afterhourspublications.com

MAKE IT LAST

CHAPTER ONE

NAOMI

Washed up. Has been. Past her prime. All the phrases that have been used to describe me and my acting career. After a while, you tend to get used to it. No one is to blame. Well, many are, but complaining won't change the nature of the beast that says that a man in this industry can work till he's wheeled out, with wrinkles and all. However, a female actress, no matter how great her talent, has a limited shelf life. I faced the hard facts that it's a man's world in Hollywood a long time ago. Being 41 years young is a death sentence in the industry.

I shift in my seat and brush off the imaginary lent on my skirt, as I listen to the conversation taking place behind me.

"Why is she so important? Who is she?"

"Lord, you can't whisper. Honey, don't make me revoke your all-access pass to the cookout. Who the hell is *that?*" The woman repeats in shocked awe. "You're kidding me, right?"

"No really, I don't know who she-"

"You can't call yourself black if you never saw *Poetic Justice, Love Jones,* and *Jason Lyrics.*"

"She wasn't in none of those," snorts the cinnamon-colored skin girl.

"No, but she put up funds to make it happen, but her movies were big hits that came out around that time, too. *Going Thru?* Remember it was a movie about five girls living in the hood? The two cousins, the twins…that was her," the girl with the neat two-strand twists explains.

"Shit, I love, *love* that movie," exclaims her friend with a new fondness of me in her tone.

I listen, while the two go down my large list of movie credits, as they mimic some of my lines here and there. Lifting my head a little higher, I stare at my reflection in the wall of mirrors before me. Starting out as a child actress, I've been through a lot of shit. Luckily, the amount of melanin in my skin that darkens my pigmentation to its ebony hue doesn't show it. From being pimped out by my parents who loved the money my acting brought, to going broke at the age of seventeen because of their spending, to building myself back up after turning eighteen to become one of the biggest names, to finally hitting rock bottom with a crack pipe clutched in my hands, I've had my share of hurt, abuse, and failures.

No, I'm not shocked to hear the whispers of those that see me. Hell, I would be amazed, too, if I saw a person that I swore was dead walking around. Yet, here I am. I've spent most of my entire 30s in and out of rehab. Then at 38, I started casting my line out for work. I didn't fool myself into thinking it was going to be easy. To do so would have been a big crushing blow to my fragile mind. No longer the diva with an ego, I took the small roles, the walk-ons, the cameos from those that I knew were throwing me a bone. Maybe to watch me crash and burn, or to see if I still had it.

Well, baby...I still got it. I crushed every role. I'm on set, on time with lines memorized and even those of my co-workers, too. The work ethics that I lacked in my privileged youth, I brought with me to every job. So much so, that no matter the size of the role or how it was written for my character to blend into the background, I shined to the point that I stole the scene.

If I was the thieving maid, I made you want to see me get away free. If I was the old mother crying over her bullied son, I made you feel my pain. If I was the one that really pulled the trigger on that episode of Law and Order; SVU, I made you understand and even question if I should be sent away for life. On screen for five minutes, thirty or an hour, I would in trance viewers to the point that all the other talents standing before the camera faded away.

Thankfully, I didn't piss away to the point of losing my gift, unlike I did with my money. The years of fucking, drinking, traveling, snorting, then smoking crack ate up all my cash like it did my edges. When my younger sister finally found me living in a hostel, I was so ashamed. I didn't want to go with her, but my will was too weak to deny her. After all, Sali didn't have to care. She could have left me in her rearview mirror like so many others had. She had been smart enough to use the door I had opened to make a connection of her own which led to her creating her own scouting and casting business. Yet, there she was, rescuing me.

A person never would believe that they would ever be in such dire straits. Oh, now as I look back, I can pinpoint the time, place, and what I was doing which put me on the road of destruction. Then, when you're in the moment of realizing your life is fucked, all you can do is send up a weak prayer to be saved. My time of clarity was while I glared at the falling down ceiling in a rust-covered bathroom. I was squatting over a chipped toilet to pee. My hand shook, as I clutched the balled-up piece of newspaper that was going to serve as my toilet paper. Not two-ply, but good enough.

It was when I looked down to find the newsprint streaked with a green discharge that I felt my heartbreak. The constant biting of the crabs that had made a home in my pubic hair didn't rattle me as much as a bad case of gonorrhea did, and the fact that I was so far down the rabbit hole that I had started hoeing myself out to keep my habit going. If I had that STD, did I have HIV? Did it even matter when I didn't have the strength to get myself out of this hell hole?

"Save me, God."

I whispered that cry in the bathroom. I chanted it while I cooked a piece of crack rock over a bent spoon before shooting it up. I cried it silently, as I laid with my face down and ass up in the air while I took a faceless dick in the ass to ensure I'll get another hit once I came down from that high. Some things can be cured with a shot or a pill, such as my case of the clap and crabs...while others can only be hid behind a smile and a pretty face.

"Hey, you ready?"

I blink myself back into the present to find Sali's dazzling smile beaming down on me.

"Took all that to prime the pump?" I huff, as I get to my red bottom feet.

"Don't think that way."

"Ah, but it's true," I pause to straighten my shoulders. Making sure my smile hasn't slipped, and my pretty face didn't show the fear raging inside, I nod, "Shall we?"

"Okay, Kenny is in the room and two other big wigs. Ken is on board, but the others- "

"Are young bucks that got their chairs at the table through their daddys," I say, cutting her off.

"Sad to say, you know the game hasn't changed that much, sis."

"No, it hasn't," I sigh.

"Hey," she comments, as she squeezes my hand, "You've paid your dues for the last four years. It's time to strike," she hisses.

Not giving me a chance to reply, her flat palm pushes the door open.

"Naomi Henson," gushes Ken.

"Kenneth," I chuckle back.

I'm determined to give the young director the respect due to him.

"Shit, black don't crack," he moans in my ear, as he embraces me a bit too long for my taste.

"Thank you for the compliment," I respond while pushing on his hard chest.

"Yes, well...this is Justin and Nathan, two of the producers of the movie," he introduces.

The men don't even have the gall to stand to shake my hand. In their eyes, they already have written me off.

"Ken and Sali were pitching you for our new movie. To be honest, I really don't think you are the right fit for the demographics we want to appeal to."

Justin must be booked for a BJ because he wastes no time getting down to business.

"What he's trying to say is-"

"I don't need an interpreter to get what he's saying. So, the part of-"

The sound of the door opening creates a wave of silence in the room. My eyes widen slightly, as I'm sure the others in the room did, too. Knees bump the underside of the long, wooden conference table when we all try to stand to our feet.

"Sit, sit! I'm not Jesus," grumbles the bald, tall man.

His long, fit legs eat up the carpeted floor, as those behind him struggle to keep up with his energy.

"Mr. Wisener," breathes Kenneth and Justin.

"Dad," snaps Nathan.

"Good to know you still recall who I am, the fucking CEO of this company," snarls Wisener. "Get the hell out of my seat."

"But we're carrying on a meeting," cries Nathan, as he stumbles to do as he is told.

"You have no business in here." Now at the head of the table, "Do you even know who this beautiful creature is?" his father questions. "My God…just look at her," he moans, while glancing at me. "Her talent…her body, shit her looks, oh the dreams I've had of you and…Fuck, forget I said that," he pleads as he runs his palm down his face. "No disrespect, please. I don't need to catch a case," he explains, as his cheeks redden under his tan skin. Breaking eye contact with me, "Move out of the way," he snaps at the two men. He rolls the leather chair back. "Stinking up the office with all that goddamn fruity hair gel. Get a juice box and sit in the corner," he orders, before he sits down. "Everyone, sit…please."

Taken back, I slide into the chair. In the seconds of the exchange, I was able to recover from seeing him. It had been years, and even then, I was never actually in his presence, just lucky to be at the same party or restaurant as him. The man is a legend in the movie industry with the Golden Touch. To be in a movie released under him is like getting the blessing of all of the other top named studios. It's the reason why Sali's been making calls and cashing in favors all month long to get me a seat in the room. It didn't matter that the movie is so left field with a part that was small, to say the least. Having my name on the credits and being in the big lights was all I'm aiming for.

Austin Wisener rocks in his chair for a few more seconds before he's ready to talk.

"Ms. Naomi Henson...what an honor," he starts.

"Actually, that should be my line," I smile.

"Bullshit," he gushes. "I have no talent. My ass gets kissed because of my position, but you...*you* are the total package. You are what the other younger African American actresses need to be striving to be."

I lick my lips to keep from speaking that I must be high or drunk.

"Mag, my sister...she's a big fan, she's taped all of your appearances over the last four years. She saw you sitting in the lobby and came to find me, thank God," he pauses to look at Kenneth, "I approve your rewrites," he announces.

"Really?! This is gonna be huge!" The director exclaims.

"I agree. I'm happy I stumbled upon your requests," mumbles Austin, as he glances over his shoulder at his son and his friend. "This movie is capable of being more than a clown show. It should be serious, well casted, and made to be a contender...and it will with our leading lady."

My head snaps back and forth between Kenneth and Austin. I'm confused. I couldn't have heard him right. A lead role?

"I'm lost," I reply. "I thought I'm here for a supporting role as the manager."

"Oh, no, no, not anymore. See, I submitted a new version of the movie once Sali put your name in the hat for casting. The movie is going to be more of an exploration, of hardships, struggles while showcasing the world of the black rodeo."

Kenneth is talking too fast, or am I in shock that I'm having trouble keeping up?

"No, not anymore. The movie is going to be more than a guy trying to pay off his debts by entering the white world of rodeo. That's what these two wanted to do. They wanted a few dumb laughs by tight casting instead of taking the subject to make it something great. Did you know the west wasn't all white, and the first real cowboys were actually black? Oh, yeah...there is a movement with blacks competing and winning. The first man to ever win the Kentucky Derby was Oliver Lewis in 1875. I didn't know that. Did you know that?" Austin presses.

All I can do is shake my head weakly.

"It's in our blood," nods Kenneth. "That's why I was hoping for a serious movie instead of the typical black film with us being paraded as clowns. You heard of the Bill Pickett Invitational Rodeo that tours nationwide?"

"Yes, and you...Naomi, are going to share top billing on this one. The part of mother/trainer was written for you," chimes Austin.

"Oh...I-I don't ride. I have no-"

"You'll learn," promises Austin, as he leans on the table. "Listen to me. I know my business. This movie is your comeback role. I don't know what you went through out there on the streets, but whatever it was has changed you and your approach to the craft. I've seen the changes from then and now. Before you were good, but in a Vivica Fox, Robbin Giviens kinda way. This role here will let you show yourself in an Angela Basset, Viola Davis, Ms. Tyson, Diahann Carroll way...full of emotions...Oscar-winning role."

"Holy shit," I sigh in dumbfounded awe.

I want to tuck my head and run. Yeah, I came to him for work, but never did I think such a life-changing role would be placed in my lap. Am I really *that* good? I mean, can I pull this off? I place my hands in my lap to keep the others at the table from seeing them shake. Salis sees, though.

"I'll do it."

My mouth, my words paint an entirely different picture than of the one that's causing my heart to be lodged in my throat.

"Yes," laughs Austin. He gives Kenneth a high five. "Leave Naomi's training to me. I know a guy that will teach you everything you need to know. You'll be roping and riding like a pro in no time at all. This is day one. I've already made some calls to a few actors and actresses that are on board. All they need is the revised script. I'll leave the location of the other actors training up to you," he says to Kenneth. "Naomi is to get special treatment. I don't want the distraction of others fucking up her getting this part down packed," explains Austin as he gets to his feet.

I'm still caught like a deer in high beams. I can hear the voices, see the mouths moving, but nothing can get past the ringing in my ears.

"Hey, I'm with you every step of the way."

Wide eyed, I look into Sali's face.

"I can work anywhere. I'm coming with you, so just breathe, okay?"

"Okay," I whisper, as I swallow hard. "What just happened?" I wonder, as I clutch her arm.

"Life, opportunity, answer to prayer, reaping what you've sown over the last four years, all of the above, is what just happened, sis," she answers. "And you're ready."

She finishes by answering the question on the top of my tongue.

"We all see it. Now, it's time for you to forgive yourself and believe it, too."

I'm speechless as she walks towards the others in the room. The fact that Wisener produces the contract is proof that this shit is actually happening. Under the table, I'm wringing my hand raw.

Remember to smile and look pretty.

The voice in my mind speaks. Doing so has helped me fake my way through. I pray it helps me now because all the fears of yesteryears are knocking.

**

When he said the work begins now, Austin wasn't shitting. In less than 48 hours, I was packed and on a private airplane off to God knows where. Resting my head on the leather headrest, I glance out the small window, as I wonder who to thank for this or who to curse? I've yet to figure out which I should be doing. Sali's swore up and down she's as floored as I am. She admitted to knowing that Kenneth wanted to make changes to the script, but she was clueless of where I fit in it all.

Maybe it's just good karma coming my way.

God knows I sure needed it. Other than the few properties I was smart enough to put in Sali's name, I don't have shit to fall back on. All the cars, private planes, the yacht, the beach home, and sprawling mansion was auctioned off years ago or the IRS seized it for taxes. I'm cash poor. The thought of living off of my little sister didn't jive well with me, no matter what she said. I want my own. Maybe not to the level I've fallen from, but enough to put me in a modest lifestyle.

I sigh, as I glance at the revised script in my lap.

This is what I've been working towards, I remind myself.

It is! So, why am I looking a gift horse in the mouth?

You know why.

The voice in my mind sounds so different than the others that have been springing up in the hope to calm me. Yes, this voice carries a smokiness to it. It produces a twinge of excitement and danger that I've come to fear will become my downfall. My gaze shifts to the neatly placed crystal bottles in the case near the cockpit area. In those bottles, I know I could lose myself along with all the hopes and dreams...along with all the faith Austin, Kenneth, and Sali has placed in me.

"Just breathe," I whisper, as I do as I command. "One step, one second at a time. That's all that is being asked of you. Not the entire answer, just work towards the solution."

It might not be the actual words of my head doctor, but it's good enough to tear my eyes away from the liquor in the room. My hand dives into my purse to retrieve a happy pill that will give me the added strength to get through the next few hours.

"I'm still on a pusher's payroll," I chuckle, as I pop the pill and swallow.

"It's really pretty, huh?"

"Yeah," I reply, while I look out to survey the patches of green. "Tell me about this place?"

"Oh, I have pictures," sings Sali. She fumbles with her cell. "See, here," she says, while passing it over to me. "We're in Indian territory."

I notch my eyebrow. "Like in Native American?"

"This is the Great Plains, South Dakota," she points out.

"Hey, don't we have some Indian blood, too?"

"Gurl, every black person says that, but I think there is some on Mom's side. Anyway, where we're going is a ranch near the Rolling Hills of The Pine Ridge Reservation. It's Lakota lands." At my deadpan stare, "They make up one of the three tribes of the Great Sioux Nation," she adds.

"Oh, I've heard of them."

"Good. The ranch we're staying at is the Hunsaker. It's over 400 acres."

"Goddamn!" I exclaim in shock.

"That's what I'm saying. I need to trade up to some leather cowboy boots."

"Nah, you and I aren't cut out for all of this," I tease.

"Your gurl could learn," she laughs. "But it has and does everything; cattle drives, breeding horses, breaking them in..."

"So, it's an *actual* ranch, not all show?"

"That's right."

I swipe through the pictures till I reach the end. "Alright, then," I sigh, as I hand her cell back. "My ass is going to be hurting."

"*Our* asses will be hurting, but it's nothing a soak, a day off, and an aspirin won't handle," she promises.

I nod. Yes, because that's all I'm willing to do to help my aches and pains. No pain killers of any kind. The fear of addiction is just that strong that I'm willing to suffer to remain sober and free.

"We'll have the place to ourselves like Austin said. Seems the owner tends to leave during this time to move the herds, so his workers will be teaching you all you need to know. These men are trained and have won many competitions. We're in good hands," she promises.

"I have no doubt," is my response. "This is the hard part. Once this is over, it's easy sailing," I smile.

"That's right," she chimes in. "We got this."

"Of course, we do. I got your back. You got mine, and we're gonna slay this shit," I preach.

"Fuck yes!"

CHAPTER TWO

NAOMI

FOUR DAYS LATER

I bat the yellow, leather-gloved hand away. It's blocking my view of the sky. I slowly tilt my head to take in the beautiful shade of blue. Have you ever just stopped to glance up? In California, things are so rushed, but here...a person can slow down and just look in awe.

"Can you see Jesus in the clouds?"

I narrow my eyes slightly at the question.

"Nah, she's just punkin' out for the fifth time today. The answer to riding isn't in the clouds, sweetheart."

"If it was, I would have had my ex going blind staring. The woman couldn't ride dick if it came with a manual."

"It wasn't her fault. It was the size of the mount. Your bitch rode my cock just fine."

As much as it pained me to move, I roll my head to the left to take in the sight of the two men that I believe get up every day with a new plan of how to torture me. Wes and Gil, brothers and two of the trio. If you ever watched the Disney movie, *Brave*, these flesh and blood three would make the three, red-headed, cartoon brothers look like a joke. You would think that the brothers were younger than me. With their fit, lean muscled bodies, tall frames, handsome features, ink-black hair, and comedic timing, yet they were actually older than my 42 years of age.

Even now, I can't help the smile, then laugh that rattles every sore bone in my body. It's been hell. I won't lie. From day one, these three assholes have been dragging me, forcing me to do all the damn work. Here I thought my training was going to be more of a City Slicker goes country. You know, the broad strokes, riding lessons, teach me how to look convincing in front of the camera, that kinda shit. Hell nah, instead, it's been a death boot camp of early 4am calls to rise, feeding of the horses and cattle, shoveling shit, riding, and today getting on the back of a horse that I know can't be broken in. I don't care what Wes and Gil claimed. The way that mare bucked and threw me has me convinced the two are getting their laughs at my dumbass expense.

"That's it, Sali. Now, give the horse a bit more lead."

I grind my teeth at the shouts of praise Graham, the missing brother, heaps on my sister.

Our training", is what she had said. Well, I would love to have the training that consists of easy riding, no shit shoveling, sly rubs on the ass, and teasing stares.

"Come on, Princess. Get your ass up."

This time, I'm not given the chance to refuse the leathered hand. Wes jerks me to my feet by my arm.

"Oh, your body hurts?" he asks in a babyish tone.

"Best thing is to ignore it. Push right through it," suggests Gil.

"Fuck y-"

"Oh, that's an extra ten minutes in the stables," snaps Wes, cutting me off.

Flabbergasted, my jaw drops. "What does me working in the barn have to do with training for my role? This isn't the all-black remake of the Karate Kid," I growl.

"Oh, I would watch that. Wouldn't you?" asks Wes, completely ignoring my anger.

"I don't know. I mean, who black could pull off Mr. Miyagi?" wonders Gil with a rub of his hairless chin.

"Fuck this bullshit," I bark.

The dry dirt creates clouds around my feet, as I shuffle away.

"So, that's it!" shouts Wes. "You gonna quit?"

"Told you she wasn't cut out for it. A fucking film about a black rodeo...come on, bro. Just pay up," demands Gil.

I should stop to cuss them out for placing bets, but at the moment, I don't care. My head is in overload. With every step, I try to calm the screaming within.

No! Don't do this. If I give up, I'll lose everything, let everyone down. I'll never work again.

The anxiety attack comes on like a freight train. My fist clutches my chest in an attempt to steady my breathing. From a shuffle, I break into a run. All I'm focused on is the third story window of my room. So much so, that I don't even see the mountain that springs up before me. The collision is hard, knocking me on my ass.

"Shit, I'm so, so sorry. Did I-"

"No, no," I remark, as I stand. "I need to get to my room," is all I mumble, as I sidestep to continue my mad dash for the house.

"Sorry!"

I hear the deep voice shout once more, but I'm on a mission to keep my shit together, and my pills are all I have to do so.

ZAHN

I stand rooted in place to watch the short woman run for the house. Someone should have told her that her wig wasn't going to last in the plains heat. The hairpiece was hanging on for dear life. I shrug off the meeting, before I turn to glance at the riding circle. I'm not too shocked to find Wes and Gil laughing, as they lean on the wooden fencing while they watch their brother Graham working with a black woman on the horse. I nod, as I take in her stance on the animal. I can see that she's not too confident, but she's doing a helluva job nonetheless. She was off to a great start. Austin should be pleased with her performance once everything is said and done.

"I need a big favor."

That was how he eased his way into asking me to train the leading lady for her role. Why me, is all I really wanted to ask. He knows I'm busy with my own shit. He knows I tend to stay to myself and circulate in a very tight circle of tribal friends. Why the hell would I want to deal with a whiny, city female? Even still, he was damn near pleading with me, as he told me that she needed to be trained by someone that he could trust. No doubt she's an actress he's fuckin, which is why he had such a personal interest in her performance.

Taking another glance across the distance, I'm a bit taken back. I would have never pegged her as Austin's type. The woman riding was too real, and not silicone, Hollywood fake. I wasn't close enough to tell if the curly mass piled high on her head was all hers, but just the look of being confident in her own brown skin didn't make her out to be a mark for Austin to shoot his shot at.

Whatever, I consider with an eye roll.

It's hot. I've ridden hard for the last two days to get back here, which pisses me off to no end. I'm in no mood of trying to figure out the life of another man's dick. I still had stuff to check on before I let everyone know I'm back for a few days. Once I stump down the drama, I'm packing up to meet up with the cattle drive, again.

Back on track, the hearty laughter follows me, as I walk around the side of the house towards the stables. If only I could goof off and laugh, but that's not my lot in life. No, my lot is to be lonely, to fight, and carry everyone over the finish line year after year. You would think with all the weight I bare; I would look like The Hunchbacked by now. Luckily, a man taught me how to bare it without showing the scars. I just pray that in doing so, I don't croak early before I can reap the harvest like he had.

NAOMI

A happy pill, a soak, a cat nap, and four hours later, I'm ready to take on the world. Dressed in jeans and a cotton tank top, I barrel down the stairs for the kitchen. I'm hungry as hell. It's the downside to the pills and the reason why I'm constantly in the gym. I might be aged, but the body can't show it in this line of work.

Slowing down, I envision the house in my mind. The place is huge. Coming to a fork, I try to remember if it's left or right. Hearing the whispering voices, I choose right. It doesn't take long to figure out I was wrong, but what can I say, I'm nosey. I tiptoe closer to the open archway.

"He's fuckin' pissed."

"Shit, I would be, too."

Okay, that's Wes and Gil talking.

"Well, the boy couldn't help it."

Now, that must be the old lady that's the cook, um...Rivers.

"Was he to force the boy when he isn't ready?" The old woman goes on.

"No, no, I understand him leaving the cattle drive to bring Russell home. It wasn't his time to quest. Look, it's hard enough trying to find your way with support. The boy is going it alone," says Gil.

"Humph, I blame his uppity parents. They get a little money, and our ways are no good. Now, we're the fools they want no part of. I thank the Heavens for Zahn taking the boy under his wings to pass the ways on. He'll get Russ right," praises the old lady.

"Shit, Zahn needs to worry about himself for a change instead of the Tribe. He needs to be getting *his* affairs right," suggests Wes.

"I say kill them all. Make it look like an accident."

"Rivers!" the brothers sing in unison.

Even I take a step back from the archway.

"What?! Don't act like ya'll never thought about it....and your father is the sheriff. I bet he could be made to look the other way if the deal is sweet enough," she snaps.

"I was never here," stutters Wes. "I won't be wrapped up in this shit."

"Fine, I'll handle it myself."

"No, *NO,* you won't, Rivers. Shit, all you need to be doing is cooking up food, pies, and shit...not setting up hits."

Footsteps. Quickly, I tiptoe away to find my way back to the fork and onward to the kitchen. I'm sure the old woman is just talking shit. Yet, I'm keeping my mouth closed. I don't know one rock from the next. Somebody could easily take me for a long drive to no return. This time, it isn't voices, but the smells that propels me to the place I have been longing for. A stone-cold killer with a sweet smile and can cook is all I want to know about old lady Rivers.

"Is it ready?"

My question causes Sali's head to pop up from her lab top.

"Don't know, hope so. I just sat down."

"Oh," I remark, as I lean over a wooden chair.

"I was going to go to your room, but I saw the shape you left in."

"It was rough," I grumble. "Everything hurts."

"And you got overwhelmed."

I don't confirm what she already knows. I drop my gaze. "I'm not giving up." I don't know if I'm saying it for her or for me. "Every day...it's getting better."

"That's right. Take it in small bites."

"I would love to, if the food was ready," I joke, in hopes of changing the subject.

At times, I get tired of talking about me fucking up and what I need to do. I get tired of leaning on a bottle of pills when all I want is to be whole again.

"But I'm happy you had another easy day," I mumble out of my twisted mouth.

"Hey, now...don't start that," she warns.

"Start what? It must be nice to have that hands-on, one on one training. I mean, you're learning the ropes so quickly under his *practiced* touch," I tease in a husky voice.

She pauses to take a glimpse at the doorway. "He is so damn fine. I mean, you remember those Indian Romances we would read?"

"Yeah, the books that had the man fuckin' all night long because he had the ways of the eagle or some bullshit," I jest.

"Yes, yes," she chimes. "I wanna know. I am going to find out," she pledges.

"Sure, you'll find out he's a minute man like all the others, and his dick isn't thick like a tree trunk, but let me know if I'm wrong."

"Don't be a hater," laughs Sali. "I need my shit tended to. My sex is on fire."

"Shit, I hope there's a cream for that."

Instantly, both of our heads turn towards the walk-in pantry that's tucked out of sight around the corner. I know Sali and I look like babbling idiots with our mouths moving and nothing coming out of them. Head tossed back, the man that had been standing, listening with the pantry door open, laughs hard to the point of almost dropping the items filling his arms. Still laughing, he drops the items to walk backward and lean on the counter to keep from falling.

"Your faces," he pauses to take a picture, before slipping his cell back into his jeans.

"And for the record, I don't think Graham passed the eagle training, so don't be expecting much," he chuckles with a wink. "Hopefully, more than a minute, though," he adds as an afterthought.

I'm speechless. Luckily, my eyes don't fail me, as I take in the man, still laughing under his breath while he goes about what he was doing. He's tall just like the brothers, so about 5'11 or a bit over 6'2. Lean muscles, tan, long raven black hair that stops midway down his back, but he's different. While the brothers have no facial hair, this man is sporting a 5'oclock shadow. His lips are thicker, too, and kinda makes me think of a Brad Pitt mouth.

"Your secret is safe with me," he promises, while he makes a turning of a key motion with his fingers. "This will all be ready in a few minutes. Rivers never puts enough kick in her chili," he explains, before going over to the chopping block. "So, how is training? You seem to be getting the hang of it," he says with a quick glance over his shoulder at Sali.

That's fine. Let him talk to her while I try to get my shit straight. She's having a hard time talking, too.

"Um, y-yeah, I'm going okay…no pro or anything," she manages at last.

"Well, you're not used to this way of life. This ranch is all I know, but you're in good hands," he promises, as he strolls over to the pot to add his own ingredients.

"Yeah, *she's* in great hands, while I'm stuck scooping piles of shit and washing animals," I complain.

Placing the lid on the pot, "Why would you be doing that? That has nothing to do with riding and roping," he frowns.

"Please tell dumb and dumber that, because that's what they're making me do to see if I'll crack."

"Really?!" he questions. "Well, fuck off, is what I would do. It's not like you need to learn any of this shit," he shrugs.

"What the hell are you doing near my pots?"

"Making your shit worth eating," he teases back, as he steps back for Rivers to reclaim her space at the stove.

"Making it taste like bulls nuts, you mean," she grumbles, as she snatches the spoon from his hands. She makes a good show of tasting and frowning. "You always have to fuck things up. Go sit down."

Not fazed, he plants a kiss on her cheek before walking away.

Fingers bite into my shoulders. I've told him how much I hate that shit. I feel no remorse when my elbow connects with his thigh.

"Where was that fight today?" hisses Wes, as he hobbles to the side of my chair.

"In the goddamn dust and dirt after the horse threw me for the fourth time."

"A horse threw you?" Mr. Stanger asks.

The energy in the room instantly shifts.

"It threw her *four* fucking times, and you were still putting her on the mount?" he growls. Pausing, he scrubs his face with his open palm. "What horse?" he goes on to question with his hands on his hips.

"Everything was under control," promises Gil.

Oh no, buddy. I wasn't going to let these two downplay shit. If this guy was going to get in their asses, I wanted to make sure he stuck his boot in real good.

"What did you joke...bruiser, punisher..." I try to answer.

"Is she all white with brown spots on the ass?" he asks in a rush.

"Yes. Is she broken in?"

He doesn't answer me. He's too busy fucking Wes and Gil up with his angry glare.

"Why the fuck...what would possess you to try her on that goddamn horse? And no, she isn't rideable... hasn't been since mounting her with a steed went wrong," he growls.

"Leave it to dick to mess with your head," I mumble under my breath.

He pauses for a second to look at me, before going back to bitching the brothers out.

"Well?" he snaps. No one makes a move. "I should fire your dumbasses. *Train,*" he shouts with a loud clap of his hands. "That's all, one thing...that's all you had to do, *train,*" he growls, flashing straight, pearly teeth, as he balls his hands into fists. "What if she broke something?"

"She wasn't going to break anything. Look at her," demands Wes. He picks up my arm and lowers it. "See, nothing broke. She's fine."

"We had a rope on the horse. We aren't stupid," speaks Gil.

"You are stupid. Austin sent her to be trained."

Why is he pointing at Sali? She must be thinking the same thing by the way we exchange glances. I open my mouth, then shut it again. I'm not about to step in the middle. It would only take him snapping at me the wrong way for me to go off.

"I don't have time for all this bullshit. I have a drive I need to get to."

"You mean you *want* to cattle drive instead of taking care of your business right here."

The sound of the spoon striking the marble countertop makes Sali and I jump. All eyes gravitate to Rivers while the man just stares ahead.

"Are you going to pass on the festival, too, because you're running away instead of using your teeth to rip out a throat or two?" she shouts.

"You would disrespect me by discussing things in front of outsiders?"

Finally, he turns slowly to give the old woman a taste of what she's hoping for. No fear shines in her brown eyes.

"If it will help you find your manhood, yes," she hisses, as she leans into the space between them.

Old lady Rivers ain't no joke. If I wondered if she was talking shit about bumping someone off, I have no doubts now. Suddenly, the man turns away.

"I'll show you all you need to know in two weeks. It will be hard, but I won't kill you."

Again, he's talking to Sali, instead of me. I tap her leg under the table to let her know to let it go. She nods. Without a word, he marches out of the kitchen.

"Oh, let him go. He knows I'm right," screams Rivers, as she walks to gather the plates.

"Well, it needed to be said. I just wasn't going to be the one to say it," admits Graham, as he takes the seat next to Sali.

"We still have jobs, right?" asks Wes.

"Of course. If Zahn hasn't done it long before now, he isn't going to do it over us having a little fun," chuckles Gil, while he hands me my plate full of food.

The sight of food combined with the drama we weren't paying for made me a bit slow in connecting the dots. Sali got to the punchline faster than me.

"Hold up," she gasps while gripping my arm. "I think he...is he the owner of this place?"

"For now, he does," sasses Rivers. "If he wants to keep it that way, he's gotta be willing to spill blood."

Taking his seat, Wes gives the old woman a warning with his eyes. "Yeah, that's Zahn Ewings...big man on campus.

CHAPTER THREE

ZAHN

With the force of the anger, I try so hard to control, my fist goes through the barn wall. Not satisfied, I make another gaping one next to it, then another until I lose all feeling in my hand. What the fuck does that old woman want me to do, huh? I'm trying all I can to keep the peace while honoring my Father's dying wishes. Well, that's not entirely true. The old man told me to fight and not to give up one grain of sand, not one blade of grass. That's what he said. It's been me that's hoping to achieve the goal while not having to destroy the family.

Comical...the word, Family. You may see it as a collection of like-minded people, all loving on one another, looking like one another, while mine is made up of a whore, a bitchy slut who wants to fuck me, a brother that wants me dead, and none that remotely care about me or resemble me in any damn way. I never knew the reason why my Father picked me to add to his family. With one daughter born, and my guess, a wife that really wasn't interested in having another child at the time, he brought me home. Maybe it was to show his love for the Tribe by adopting a castaway. One thing is for sure, the threat of having everything left to a red skin was enough to get his wife, my adoptive Mom, to lay on her back to breed him another child, a boy.

Imagine my shock to find out that at the end of the day, the old man gave them one more, Fuck You, by leaving me the ranch; all 400 acres, the houses on the lands, and all the animals. I was ready to take whatever money was piece off to me and move the hell on. Yet, I was left standing as the richest man in the goddamn county, if not state. I mean, it made sense to me on paper for things to go down as it did. I was the only one that showed any love for the land and the people that made a living off of it.

When my adoptive father couldn't do as he was used to, I stepped in while his kids toured the world on his dime. Neither one could tell a difference from a bull or a calf. All they wanted was the money to be deposited on time. No, I shoulder the weight, the burdens of keeping things going. When things got hard for the Tribe, I opened up the land to allow them to hunt and farm like the ways of old. How was I supposed to know that in doing so would breathe life into our dying people by giving them pride, once again? It was like a shot of electricity to waken the dry bones of the Elders and even the youth that wanted to re-connect. It also added another thing on the list that I have to not only maintain but another case against me, too.

The fact that a red man is controlling all this power and wealth was bad enough. Now, he's helping others to come up, too. Well, fuck that! We can't have these red skins having pride in their culture...or money. And so, the harassment started. Heads of prized cattle went missing or were being gutted in the fields. Crops that yielded a thousand-fold before are now dying in the ground due to airborne pests. Then on the left, I have my family with their teams of pale-faced lawyers that want to carve it up and sell it all in fear that I might die and leave it all to the Tribe.

The sounds of the horses draw me deeper into the barn.

"You silly ass horse," I grumble.

I still can't believe the foolishness of Gil and Wes. I'm sure they still took precautions, but anything could have happened. The desire of a laugh at that woman's expense wasn't worth the trouble.

I shake my head as I enter the stall. The gun-shy mare stumps the earth while eyeballing me.

"You know who I am. Stop that shit," I demand.

Reaching up, I stroke the side of her face to make her calm down.

"Like it or not, you're going back into the field. I've given you time to heal, but you know it has to happen," I coo. "I'll do better in the picking this time, okay," I whisper.

"That's why I love you so much."

That one word being uttered by a woman, any woman makes me freeze in my tracks.

"Oh, when did that happen…loving me?" I question, still stroking the mare.

"I've always loved you, Zahn."

This time, I do glance over my shoulder to take in the lanky female. She knows how to show off her best assets. Her tea tinted hair is braided back to bring attention to her high cheekbones, while the low cut of her shirt is giving me full access to her full tits. Birthing two babies has blessed Morgan with one hell of a rack. Too bad some of the extra wasn't placed in her ass, too.

"How you know I was back?"

"You know how word spreads on the wind."

She doesn't wait for an invite. She twists on in, sticking to the wall to place two tin mugs and the bottle of brandy in her hand on a bale of hay. I watch while she pours one mug full, before moving the hover over the other.

"Bring the bottle."

"I need you to be able to get it up," she sasses, while coming my way.

I rake my eyes down her body, as I determine if I even want to fuck her or not. One deep swig from the bottle and I think maybe. Three more swigs and a refill of her mug, and I'm thinking, hell yeah. Her hands that were once content on my chest travels lower.

"God, you're always hard," she moans.

"You have a condom?"

"No, but-"

My sharp eyes register that I'm not that drunk to go deep-sea diving without protection. I've too many women try and fail to slap me with a kid. At 48 years old, I wasn't going to fall prey to the pussy trap.

Getting to my feet, "You know what that means…or you can leave."

Morgan doesn't hesitate to drop to her knees in the dirt in front of me. I actually prefer it this way. At the end, she'll either swallow or spit in the dirt for me to cover with more dirt later. My head rolls back, as I take one more drink from the bottle. I close my eyes to focus on her mouth sucking on my dick. Where she is lacking in the pussy game, she makes up of it with her deep throating skills. I glance down to witness her take all 10 inches till her lips brush against my curly pubes.

"Yess," I hiss, as I pump my hips.

Slowly, the cool night air touches my length when she backs away. Closing my eyes, I wait to be drawn back into her wet warmth. Three seconds. Five seconds. Finally, I crack an eye to receive the shock of my life.

"Put your damn pole away."

My hand fumbles to cover myself.

"And you, bitch…save some of that for your husband," grunts Rivers, as she tights her grip on Morgan's hair to shake it like a sack of potatoes.

"Fuck, you're back with Carl?" I ask in a rush.

My dick damn near catches the gold, metal teeth of my zipper.

"Oh, she didn't tell you the happy news?" sorts the old woman, before she pushes Morgan out of the stall, head first. "They were just down in the bar yesterday night, all hugs and shit."

I send up a silent prayer for Rivers' bossy ass coming to find me. Yeah, I've fucked Morgan, as did half the men when Carl was on one of his benders that would lead to the two splitting, but never when he was home.

"Go home to your family, Morgan. Thanks for the bottle," I gesture my head in the direction of the door.

"You'll stick that thing anywhere, huh?"

"Listen, thank you for the rescue, but I don't need-"

"I only came to make sure you ate," the old woman that I see as my grandma says, cutting me off. "Come here and eat."

Not giving me a chance to refuse, she shuffles out of the stall. My engrain desire to please my elders, or maybe the fact that I am hungry, forces me to fall in step behind her. The bags piled on top of a poorly made, wooden table has been shifted to the side to clear enough room for a bowl, a towel filled with bread, and a cold beer. Tossing my leg over an empty barrel, I plop down.

"Thanks," I grumble, sounding like a child instead of a man, as I start to eat.

We share the silence till she breaks it.

"I can feel the chill in the air. You think we'll get an early snow?"

I shrug. "If so, it won't be much, and it won't last long."

"I hope you're right," she whispers with a nod. "Any issues on the drive."

"None when I left," I reply through a mouth full of chili soaked bread.

"Don't worry about Russ too much. He's a good boy. He'll know what to do when it's time. We already know what we have to do. It's just the fear of the unknown or the pain it may cause... but choosing comes to all of us."

I raise my gaze to lock with hers. "The choice isn't as hard as you may think. There is no fear, and the pain is of no worry, either. Like you said, he already knows what to do."

I notice the slight flicker of her lips curling in the corner. This is how she and I communicate; in riddles, parables with neither one of us ever saying sorry for the harsh words spoken because we have a love that's present, but unspoken. We're too pig-headed for that mushy shit.

**

NAOMI

"Shit," I hiss, as I stab the green button on my cell to stop the constant, mellow tone voice.

I've come to realize that all the tapes, books, and gurus are all the same, spitting the same game with none of their words of wisdom working. In frustration, I dig at my neatly braided corn rolls till they hurt. Getting to my feet, I fall back into the trail I created in the well-worn rug covering the hardwood floor to pace again.

"I can do this."

I almost laugh at the sound of my voice after speaking. Who the hell am I fooling? Surely not myself. Although I know I need this shot, I honestly don't believe I can do it. Sometimes, things aren't better the second time around. Some doors are shut, opportunities are missed that never come back around, no matter how much we wish it. Then again, why should I be given this chance of redemption, huh? Yeah, I hear the words of faith from others, but if they only knew...really knew the piece of shit I really am, I wonder if they would be so vocal for my comeback.

The thing about facing the music and admitting your faults is that the tune stays with you. The harmony becomes the background sound of your life. For me, it's a song of failure, of fear that I will never be great again. It's a low beat that is easily mixed and hidden underneath the cheerful fan fair that plays for all the world to listen.

"I can do this," I repeat, a bit stronger.

I gotta shake myself. I gotta get a handle on this. Fake it till you make it.

Pausing in mid-pace, I straighten my shoulders, smile, and recite a few lines of my script. Some things never change. The raw talent I was blessed with can't be denied. I know how to make love to that camera, to make you cry, cum, or scream with emotion as you watch on in awe. I know how to split my mind and soul to become the person that's needed for the role. It doesn't matter that I have a hundred different voices yelling in my skull, I'll pop a tiny pill to level it all out.

Suddenly, I chuckle.

"The owner doesn't even know who I am."

Funny, but sad, too. It's a true reflection of the world. Face it, I'm outdated. I'm no Gab Union or Angelia Basset. I can walk the aisles of Target without anyone noticing who I am.

"But that's all gonna change...right?"

I take in my creased faced reflection in the full-length mirror. This time, it's for me. Each goal, each achievement...it's all for me.

**

I swear I had just closed my eyes. The sleep was hitting good and hard only for the alarm to chime. Reluctantly, I roll out of bed. The fact that I'm doing all this bullshit is proof that I really want to succeed. To be honest, I don't know how I've been able to dress and make my way through the still house to the kitchen every morning with only one eye open. Like always, I slide my sore ass into one of the chairs at the kitchen island to wait for the smell of coffee being placed in front of me. My head hits the granite countertop to fall back asleep as I wait. I don't know if I was out of five minutes or thirty before the aroma of coffee beans assault me.

"Thanks," I slur.

Without raising my head, I reach out to feel the warmth of the cup. Not the soft wrinkles I was expecting of Rivers, but instead rough callous. I groan in annoyance.

"I was hoping to not see your ugly faces first thing in the morning?" I grumble.

"Wow, most people don't deem me ugly until at least the third meeting."

Instantly, all sleep is gone. My head snaps up to find not Wes or Gil, but the man from last night.

"Jesus," I hiss in shock. "I'm so, so very sorry. I thought you were one of the other assholes," I try to explain.

"Oh, so you miss labeled me as ugly," he smirks.

"Lord, no," I stumble at his darkening expression. "I mean, no as in...you're far, *far* from being ugly." Suddenly, his comical expression has me tongue-tied. "What I meant to say is that you are, very, um... I-I'm going to be late," I finish in a rush.

"Late for what?" he asks, still with a smirk on his lips.

Shit, he really is fine. I mean, I noticed it last night, but not to this degree. Did he get sexier overnight? No, it's the fact that he's bathed and smelling good....and it's the hair, too. Last night it was pulled back into a long braid. Now, his inky black hair is in a messy bun on top of his head. It's now that I notice strains of gray peppering his temples.

Just how old is he, I wonder.

I know he's waiting for me to answer. Why am I having trouble answering him?

"Training" is all I manage to get out, before getting up to walk out of the kitchen. "I need dick," I mumble under my breath.

That can be the only explanation for my reaction to him. Too bad his dick and all dick are off-limits to me...well, according to my doctor. Nope, he'll just enjoy being given the current number one spot ahead of all the men I have collected to fuck me in my hottest dreams.

Suddenly, my steps slow to a standstill, as I recall something from last night.

"I'll show you all you need to know in two weeks. It will be hard, but I won't kill you."

"Crap," I grunt, as I cast my eyes over my shoulder towards the kitchen. He's my new trainer.

CHAPTER FOUR

ZAHN

I read the time on my cell like an impatient professor waiting for the bell to ring. The thing is, the bell had rung over twenty minutes ago, and the seat of one is still empty.

"Where the fuck is the girl?" I growl.

No longer willing to wait and wonder, I jump the wooden fence of the training ring to head towards the house. The idea is to start early before the sun cranks up the heat. On cue, the woman from this morning rounds the side of the house. Since she's not with the girl I'm after, I don't bother to slow my long strides in my hunt.

"I know you're used to Wes and Gil's way of fuckin' around, but my time is valuable," I belt out in the distance between us.

"I was doing the morning runs like I was told to do before coming to see you."

"Why the hell I want to see you?" I ask, as I march past her.

"Well, aren't you going to train me?"

"This isn't a two for one. I only have time for one slow foot," I toss over my shoulder.

"And *I'm* the slow foot!"

Confused, I turn around. Gone is the strange, babbling woman from the kitchen. She's been replaced with a clearly heated, tired, and pissed female with her hands on her hips.

"Okay, you are-"

"Naomi...we tried to clear that up last night, but..."

Her words trail off, as my eyes take her in. Now that I take the time to stop, she does look familiar, more so than the other girl.

"I'm sorry for the mix-up. Austin didn't give me many details about who was coming," I clarify.

"I'm sure. He's treating everything like it's a state secret," she sighs, as I gather closer to her.

I swear, she looks so damn familiar.

"The other girl is *my sister*, Sali," she explains.

My mind may be foggy, but the way my body is acting now that I'm towering over her, you would think I've fucked her a million times over. I drop my head to hide my thoughts.

"Alright, then...let's do this right. I'm Zahn Ewing, owner," I nod, with a beaming smile.

I find myself holding my breath, as I wait for her to drop her name.

"Naomi Henson, actress," she replies, with a smile of her own.

This revelation makes a lot of sense. I feel my practice smile beginning to slip.

"Is something wrong?"

Her question pulls me out of my thoughts.

"No," I promise. I make sure to keep my expression casual when I hold out my hand for her to shake. Unlike before, I don't train my eyes on her face. Instead, I allow them to examine her from head to toe. "The fault is mine," I admit, after I free her hand. "and forget what those fuckers told you. They can do their own work."

Shit, how could I have not known who she is? Yeah, she's a bit older. Sure, she's been off the scene till more recently, but she's still the person I would beat off to in my early twenties. Lord, I'm getting hard thinking about the sex scenes she did in that cop movie I watched on a daily basis back in the day. She showed full bush in that film.

"You alright?"

"Yes, I was just remembering something," I smirk. With a wave of my hand, I signal for her to head for the ring.

Yes, how could I have not recognized you? I wonder, while I follow the sway of her hips ahead of me. *The son of a bitch*, I chuckle mentally when I think of Austin sending her my way without a heads up.

Once at the ring, "Let me see what you've learned," I order, as I hop the fence to get back into the practice area. "This is Brook. She's well ridden, so she won't give you too many issues."

I take note of the confidence she displays, as she approaches to hold out her hand for the horse to get her scent. She waits for the nestling, before she strokes Brook. Good. All good. I say nothing for a full minute to give her and the horse time to get used to each other.

"Ready?"

Now, I see it. It lasts for a second, but the look of fear is there before she hides it. It's normal. We're not dealing with a small pooch. A horse can fuck up even the most trained.

Without a word, Naomi strolls to Brook's side, places her foot in the stirrup, grabs the saddle and hoist herself up. I mentally shake my head when I begin envisioning her wide-legged and straddling my hips.

"How does it feel?"

Lord, I need help. Even my question has a hidden meaning behind it to feed my twisted humor.

"I feel sore and uncomfortable."

I can't look at her and keep a straight face.

"I mean, I'm not used to so much between my legs."

Jesus, this woman, I think, as I pretend to tighten the straps to hide my expression and my wicked chuckle.

"But I'll get used to it," she promises.

I wonder if she notices the moan that coats her statement? I'm sure her reasons for it aren't the twisted ones I have in my mind.

"Let me see how you ride, Naomi."

While her moan was innocent, the thickness in my tone which deepens my voice isn't, nor is the look I convey in the depths of my eyes when she glances down in confusion. It only takes a second for her to realize what just happened. Her face goes deadpan, she rolls her eyes, and I laugh.

"Seriously?" she drawls.

Walking backward, I watch as she puts the horse in motion. I don't know what was going on during the time I was gone, but training wasn't it. Her form is bad. Her commands are non-existing, and that's just the few things I see in the first five seconds.

Can I still teach her in two weeks to get back to the cattle drive and away from the other shit that's brewing here? Of course. Will I, is the question? Of all the places Austin could have sent Naomi, he sent her to me. Not by mistake, I'm sure.

It takes all my focus to do just that. To focus on the task and not the woman or the fantasies I stopped having by the time I reached my thirties.

"That's enough," I say in a rush, as I jog over to grab the dangling reigns.

Quickly, I move Brook to the side to give Naomi room to army crawl to safety after being thrown. The dust and dirt clinging to her brown skin is a testament to the hard work she's put in the last two hours.

"Break."

It's not a question. I won't give the foolish woman the option to continue on as Wes and Gil had. Her desire to learn for a role is going to get her killed.

"I don't think horses like me," she grumbles, as she rolls up to sit on her ass.

"Maybe you should seek a part as a sheep farmer," I suggest in an attempt to lighten the mood.

Her rapid breathing is giving me a cause to worry.

"Just breathe, okay? You'll get it."

"I nee-need something to dr-"

"Oh yea," I cut her off. "You're not used to this dry heat," I say, while tearing into the white Styrofoam cooler safely out of the way.

Not glancing inside out of fear of taking my eyes off of her, I grab the first thing my hand touches. Naomi freezes, causing me to examine what I'm holding.

"Beer?" I say, wondering why Gil would have put that in the damn thing.

"I can't...don't drink," she informs me with a touch of her fingertip to a sobriety charm attached to her bracelet.

"Oh, fuck," I snap. I pull the glass bottle back, as if I had just offered a priest a viewing of porn on my cell. In a second, I produce a bottle of water.

I say nothing while I watch her like a hawk. Her long, thin, shaking fingers can barely obey her command to pop open the childproof top to gain her access to the pills within. When she does, she swallows it down with a swig of cold water, as if she has been granted a few more moments of life, thanks to it.

"Listen, I commend you for wanting to work and all, but maybe this role is a bit too much for you. Your health is much more important."

The chuckle she gives me is raw with too many emotions. The fact that she decides to not look me in the eyes says a lot.

"There's nothing wrong with my body," she answers, before tapping the side of her head. "I just need a moment."

Once again, I glance at the pill bottle still clutched in her hand. I nod while picking up the beer that was meant for her.

"Congrats, by the way," I remark. I tip the beer in the direction of her charm. "How long?"

The tension creasing her face relaxes a bit. I feel a tingle in my loins due to the slight smile on her full lips.

"Three years and some change," she replies, beaming with self-pride.

"Addiction to the drink is a common thing with my people."

My confession is rewarded with her brown eyes on me.

"You would think that finding out how it was used as a weapon against them during the time of expansion would have taught them to stay away. Then again, look at my dumbass," she finishes in a mumble.

"Well, some habits are hard to break. Even when we know the dangers, we still walk across the street," I add with a shrug. I know I shouldn't ask, but my desire to get closer to her pushes me. "And those?"

It takes her a little longer to answer. "For stress...anxiety," she whispers. "It's a very common thing in Hollywood."

I nod, as I keep my expression void. "Well, people cope in different ways."

I don't miss the arching of her eyebrow at my comment. I might have come off sounding like a douche bag, but I have my reasons.

"I'm ready to get back to work," she announces while getting to her feet.

Now, it's my turn to stare.

"Is that your way of putting me in my place, Naomi?"

My signature smirk is on my face, but trust me, I'm far from being happy.

"Of course not. Just like I'm sure you weren't judging me."

I narrow my gaze. "I'm shocked at how much of a piss poor actress you've become with age. Are you sure you don't want to spend time in front of the mirror getting those lines down?" I cut her off, before she can get her next word out. "I wasn't judging you, Naomi. All I was doing was offering another way to cope that didn't involve lining a doctor's pockets for the rest of your life. You're not healed if all you do is treat the symptoms with one thing or another," I explain, as I motion to her bracelet than to the pill bottle.

NAOMI

What the fuck is this? Did I miss the inner healing retreat sign on the way to the ranch? I bite down on my lip to keep what I really want to say from spewing out. Who the hell does...does, shit! I've forgotten his name.... *Dances With Wolves*, think he is trying to read me like that? I'm doing better than I've ever done. Sure, I can't go a day without taking my meds. Yeah, I've admitted in the darkness of night after having a panic attack that there has to be another way...and after years of therapy, I've yet to have that breakthrough that would calm me and bring me inner peace, but fuck him, all the same.

"I really want to continue," I stress again at his back.

"I was born on the plains, not the *African* plains. I don't work in the direct heat if I don't have to," he responds, while going toward the horse.

"That didn't stop Wes and Gil," I point out.

"Don't ever compare me to those fools," he remarks. "They were clowning you, Naomi," he continues, as he grabs the lead to head for the opening on the far side of the wooden fence. I have to power walk just to keep up. "They know damn well not to be working out in the full of the sun. We'll pick back up around…5, maybe 6."

"What am I to do till then?"

Okay, what's with that look? You know the kind. When you can tell that a person is itching to say something off-colored but by sheer power alone, they resist. It's in the upturning of the curves of his lips. It's in the way his light brown eyes warm, as he stares down at me. His slick mouth is a dirty one.

"Nevermind, Dances With Wolves," I huff with a speak to the hand.

Electric shock. That's the only thing that comes to mind at the sensation which travels down my spine and settles in the pit of my stomach. Head toss back, his neck exposed, the deep tenor of his laughter rings out. I'm stunned. I'll admit knowing that he's willing and wanting is wreaking havoc on my dusty pussy. Even still, I can't fuck things up by spending time on my back or on my knees, when I should be on the saddle.

"What the fuck you just called me?"

I hear his question. I wonder why he has to close the gap between us to ask it, though?

"Well, I can't remember your name," I reply, annoyed by everything he does and says.

"Um," he chuckles. "And you improvised?"

Far away, in dem lighting, in the brightness of day, dirty, clean, hair up or down…this damn man is a lady killer. That's just what he's doing. With a tilt of his head, he's watching me, sizing me up. What the hell is he thinking?

"I'll let you do whatever you're going to do," I announce, as I back away.

"No."

It's not his commanding voice that stops me. It's the fact that my feet are no longer on the ground that does the trick. As if I weigh just a paper bag, he grabs me by the waist to place me back on top of the horse.

"You can come with me. It will give you a chance to study my form on the saddle," he explains.

It seems like only a few minutes for him to walk to the barn to re-emerge riding the large black stallion I've taken great pains to stay away from. Here I thought he was joking that this was part of the training. Yet, he's saying something important, but all I can do is pretend to be listening. When, in fact, I'm watching his lips move, not hearing a word.

This isn't a movie. Attraction isn't this strong or instant, I chastise myself in hopes that I'll snap out of it.

He isn't sweating, I notice with amazement when my gaze drops to his chest.

The white t-shirt that's stretching to cover his large muscle chest under the lightweight, long-sleeved grey shirt is void of moisture. Mindlessly, I remove the scarf from my back pocket to wipe the sweat from my neck. This heat is no joke.

Longingly, I steal a glance of the house in the distance, I know it's nice and cool under the roof. I should have taken his offer to break for the day till it got cooler in the evening.

"It won't be so bad once we reach the forest."

He must have read my mind. Lord, I hope he only got the bits about the weather and not my thoughts about him. My eyes dart back up to find him giving me that mischievous smirk that I find annoying and unnerving. He wasn't lying, though. Once we made our way to the cluster of trees to enter, the temperature dropped. Not having to actually do anything except hold on to not fall off the saddle, I surveyed the land while trying not to stare too much at the man leading me. Broad shoulders, lean muscles, I watch as his strong legs grip the sides of the monster of a horse to give gentle commands to the four-legged beast. His long, tanned fingers didn't even have to hold the reins of his horse or mine that were secured around his saddle horn.

In that instant, I can see why my sister was so taken with Graham. Old Dances With Wolves seems to be the embodiment of every myth and lore that sold millions of romance novels.

"I told you to *watch* me ride, not to fuck me with your eyes."

His comment out of the blue damn near knocks me from the horse. The mare underneath me must have felt the tensing of my body. In response, she stalls and begins to pound the earth.

"Calm down, Naomi," he chuckles at my expense. "There's nothing wrong with liking what you see," he winks, while effortlessly getting the horseback under his trance. "You have to remember that a horse isn't a car. It has feelings, which means it can sense feelings, too. Just like you or me, they will react."

I say nothing, but nod. All I want him to do is to get this train moving without pointing out that I was caught ogling him again. He might be holding back the words to torture me, but him choosing to not ride in front with me bringing up the rear is even worse. Side by side, in the slowest canter I can imagine, he leads us through the trees. Is that the sound of thunder?

No, dummy. It's the sound of your heartbeat, the voice in my mind informs me.

Absentmindedly, my hand gravitates to my pills crammed in my back pocket. Knowing that they are there kinda calms me in a strange and sad way. I don't have to steal a peek to see if he saw me.

"Is it the horses, being alone with me, or just me that makes you nervous?"

"All of the above," I grumble, only to slap my mouth shut. "Why did I jus-"

"It's because you're so worked up that you are clueless to what you're doing. You don't owe me nothing. I am just a guy on a horse that's taking pleasure in flirting....and you're here to learn a new skill. Simple."

"Yes, a woman to learn a skill, not to fuck the day away," I correct.

He sighs, as if he's been wounded. I can't help but wonder if he tries to get in the pants of all the women that visit his ranch?

"Are you going to tell me after almost a week, why you don't know shit?"

I shift in the saddle. "I'm doing the best I can to-"

"It's learning to ride a horse, Naomi," he says slowly, as if I'm a dim whit. "So, why are you shooting yourself in the foot?" he presses.

This red-skinned, motherfucker.

"Watch yourself, or she might throw you."

The warning makes me try to relax my body. My head is ringing from the way I'm grinding my teeth, but the asshole is right. Getting thrown in an open space is one thing. Being thrown in the dense woods is another. My head could hit a tree trunk.

"What lawsuit did you win to own all this land? Or did the government hand it over?"

I hate the fact that my questions seem to not faze him in the least. Instead of anger, all he does is laugh, as he slides off the saddle to walk a few yards ahead to check on something.

"Oh, this is when you read the broken twigs to tell us what's up ahead?" I joke, nastily.

Is that a hit of anger in his raised eyebrow when he glances over his shoulder to look back at me? He takes his time, as he examines a large wooden barrel, before he gets back on his horse to ride on.

"That's a corn barrel to attract deer. In a few days, the woods will be full of them for the junior hunt," he explains calmly.

"Isn't that cheating? I thought you spoke to the wind and mother nature for your food?" I sass again.

This time, I know I'm pissing him off. "I hope you're now playing the role of a bitter bitch, because I'm not the one to mess with, Naomi," he warns without taking his eyes from the unseen trail.

Cold. I mean, fucking ice cold. Not a raise in his voice... actually, it got deeper with his threat. His normal smirk transforms from joking to sinister with an odd twisting of his mouth that I would have never thought such a handsome face could do.

"I take great pride in knowing who I am and where I come from. I don't need to mail off my DNA for a report of a colored map in hopes of finding out where my people originate from to give me a feeling of belonging."

Well, he just shut me up.

How does he do that? How the fuck does he seem to always put me in my place with such ease? I can't stand it. Where the hell are his buttons? Yet, he can see me even when I'm doing my best to stay hidden behind my layers.

"I'm sorry, but you-"

"Don't say sorry if you're going to follow it up with an excuse," he interjects.

"Who the fuck are you?"

"I'm the man wondering why you're wasting my time and yours, too?"

"Know what?!" I shout. "Stop! I want off broke-back mountain. I knew this wasn't going to work. A black rodeo? Who the hell is going to pay money to see this shit?"

"Not you in the starring role. Nobody wants to see that. Whoever thought of that is a damn fool," he adds.

"I tried to tell them that. Hell, you didn't even know who the hell I was, last night. How do they expect me to carry a movie? All the money, time, the reviews…" I trail off to ride silently in my thoughts for a moment. "You got me," I admit with a shake of my head. Hearing myself say it causes my heartbeat to accelerate slightly. Suddenly, a fear overtakes me. "I-I mean, I'm sure I can-"

"Like I said, it's just us. Yeah, Austin and I are friends, but we aren't going to really throw in the towel, Naomi. Don't go into hiding after just coming out," he smiles.

Hopping off, he goes to check another barrel. I notice the creasing of his forehead when he gets back on his horse.

"Something wrong with your corn?" I ask.

"Not the corn, but still not happy with the results," he mumbles, while looking in every direction.

"The deer outsmarting you, huh?" I guess.

"They can try," he grunts. "A total of 400 acres is what I own. That's 400 reasons for people not to like me. That's also 400 reasons for people to want to fuck with me in ways that could get a person hurt."

"Oh, I understand. That's a lot of land and money for a-"

"Red skin, injun, prairie nigger? I get it just like all the rest. They just say it behind a smile or an action because of the money I control. Shit, I get it from my own family that can't stand that my old man, my adopted father, left me the land."

"I wasn't going to say all of that," I remark a bit taken back. "I would say, welcome to America, but seeing how you and your tribe was here first, well," I finish with a shrug.

I'm not shocked about the others in the area. What farmer wouldn't be jealous over all that Dances With Wolves, geesh I gotta find out this man's name, owns? Nah, it's what he said about his own family that struck a chord. Blood might be thick, but you put money in the mix and that shit might dilute real quick. Trust me, I know that first hand.

"We all have weight to bare, Naomi. There are people that are counting on me, just like they are counting on you because when you and I succeed, they do too. That pressure is a son of a bitch, trying as fuck," he ends in a whisper.

I blink at his admission. Taking in the graying strands in his head, no doubt it's from the stress of it all. The high fees of a great hairdresser hide mine, but I have my share. In spite of it all, he still carries himself with a confidence and strength that reputes all he just said.

"So, this hunt is a big deal?"

"It's a three day hunt before the start of the 5-day festival. It will be the first hunt for many of the young boys hoping to be recognized by the Tribe as men...and I host it...every year, much to the anger of those around here."

"Why the fuck should they care what you're doing?" I question.

"The same reason why taking a knee caused such a problem. The same reason why in hopes of stamping out our pride, my ancestors were forced into schools that stripped them of their language and beliefs. Some people don't like it when another culture is celebrating or when people find knowledge and strength in their past. Those same people are afraid of the outcome that they can't control. My father opened up his lands for the people on the reservation to hunt, which got a lot of people around here in their feelings, but they kept their mouth shut cuz it was him."

He didn't need to say no more, and I was happy when he got lost in his thoughts the rest of the way. It isn't even me, and I'm fuckin pissed. It's the same old story, different day, location, and group. Now that I think about it, I do remember seeing a picture in one of the many rooms in his home. I was lost, so after peeking in to realize I was in the wrong place, I backed out, but I did get a quick glimpse. I recall seeing a good looking white man standing next to a young, but a fine tanned boy. That was no doubt him. Closer to the door, there was a large painting of a blonde woman surrounded by a girl and a younger boy. If that was the rest of his family, then I know without him saying, he had one helluva life in that home. Last night, I was clueless about what was being said around the kitchen table, but things are coming together to create a pretty fucked up picture, indeed.

"On my tour, I noticed a picture of your father. He was a good-looking man," I remark, breaking the silence.

"Oh yes, Bradly Ewing was a hell-raiser," he laughs with a nod. "The pale brother to the Lakota, is what is said about him. He was the only one that saw the pains of the people. Now, he didn't return the land that his forefather took, but he made amends by paying to clean up the poisoning of the reservation's land from the dumping courtesy of the chicken farm up the road. When the wells went dry, he routed one of the properties many streams over there. He funded schools and sent many to college, gave a few business loans."

"Good looking and a saint," I comment. "And he left it all to you. In a way, he did give it back to the people," I point out.

He locks eyes with me to smile. "In a way, he did."

A smoothness enters his voice that makes it hard for me to swallow. "Hopefully, your kids will be as smart as you are," I say in a roundabout way to find out if he has any…or, better yet, a woman in his life.

Listen, I'm just being nosey, that's all. His brown eyes take on a heat and intensity while he examines my face.

"Life has a way of running away from you when all you're trying to do is survive. You never realize how much has been wasted seeing to others' needs instead of your own."

Lord, this man isn't trying to be subtle in his flirting. His gaze is hot. His voice deep and steady.

"It will be my final finger to my family to leave everything to the Tribe," he chuckles suddenly to break the sensual tension he so easily had created.

"Listen, I can see that things are getting hot around here. I don't want to add to or be in the middle of any drama," I speak.

All he does is look at me with his light brown eyes without commenting.

"You find out that I'm free to play, and then you try to run away," he replies.

Flabbergasted, my mouth becomes unhinged.

"What woman lied to you?" I grunt, refusing to look at his grinning face.

"Come on, Naomi," he teases. "asking about kids and shit. All you have to do is ask."

"Fine, I'm *asking* you to shut the fuck up," I growl.

He looks heavenwards to sigh.

The distant sound of voices gets my attention. Breaking from the trees, we're at the mercy of the hot sun above, as we enter a clearing. Near the back, left side is a huge, circler, dome-shaped building. It's bent bones exposed for all to see. To the side, in a pile, is what I can only assume to be the layers of material used to create the outer walls of the hut.

"For the record, I do remember you. Last night, my mind was elsewhere, but I know who you are...your roles. You started doing commercials as a kid. Then you acted on educational shows. Hell, I learned how to divide by twos from the *Mob Squad* episodes. But your big break, I think, was your time on *Bold and The Beautiful*. Rivers was a fan of that dumb soap opera. No one could talk during the hour it was on. Good luck getting a snack, and because I was always getting into trouble, she made me sit and watch along," he groans.

Suddenly, he stops our horses. Leaning into my personal bubble, he continues, "Then there's the collection of 5, no... 7 movies you did in your early twenties that I have committed to memory. I watched them so much...alone."

He adds that last word with a lick of his lips.

"You're not the only one...young and old that wants to fuck their crush," I say sarcastically.

Am I flattered? Hell, yeah. What I'll never tell this man, with his out of control ego, is he's the finest piece of male flesh I've caught the eye of in a long while.

"I apologize for leading you to believe that's all this is, but I promise you, it's more than that," he states.

True to what seems to be my normal in regards to this man, I open my mouth to shame myself in the worse of ways.

"I can't have sex because my therapist says I have the tendencies to become a sex addict," I blurt out.

His perfect eyebrows reach for the sky to complete his comical expression. His lips round into a large O shape, before they curve into a wide, shit-eating grin. If I wasn't so dark, I know I would be beet red with embarrassment.

"Well, it seems you need training in more areas than one, Ms. Naomi. Thankfully, I'm a jack of many trades," he promises.

"You need to stake your claim elsewhere. Maybe the next horny, brainless chick that books your services."

He tsk with a deep eye roll. "You played the prudish chick in that western. Good work, but not my favorite. Try telling me what's really clanking around in that overthinking brain of yours."

My eyes fall to the low grass underneath me. I know I shouldn't allow him the pleasure of getting under my skin.

"Are you hinting that I've peaked early?" I award him with my open stare.

He laughs for a second, then goes serious. "I'm the chief of sinners, so no judgment. Naomi, anyone that thinks you have nothing left to offer is blind. You have so much more to give on and off the screen...and last I checked, I have 20/20 vision."

I tilt my head. "Are you flirting with me, Dances With Wolves?"

"If you have to ask, then I need to pick up the intensity. Is that what I need to do?"

Yes! Move your big lips and say, YES!

"What you need to do is trot your old ass over to your friend on the phone and leave me alone," I sass.

"Lord," he moans, while he shifts in the saddle. "I can't wait to see all of the real you," he remarks, ignoring my statement.

"Zahn!"

My head finds the man in the distance wearing a police uniform shouting the name. I watch Zahn waves to the man sitting on his ATV.

"Zahn," I repeat.

Reaching out his hand, he captures mine to shake it.

"It's less of a mouthful than Dances With Wolves." Quickly, he unravels the reigns to my horse. "And much easier to moan…or maybe scream. You'll have time to practice how you're going to say my name," he suggests, as he nudges his horse away.

"I'm thinking more of a growl, like, *fuck you, Zahn.*"

In spite of my comment, I can't ignore the flutter of butterflies in the pit of my stomach.

I always was a sucker for good looks and too much confidence.

Yeah, and that never ended well.

CHAPTER FIVE

ZAHN

"Is that really Naomi Henson?"

The breathless question gives me a reason to pause. "Stop staring," I snarl. "How the hell you knew it was her before me?"

I wish to God someone would have taught the old fool how to look without being noticed. No doubt, Naomi knows she's the main topic. My father's closes friend and a second father to me puffs out his chest, knowing he got a leg up on me.

"I'm the sheriff. Of course, I knew she was here," shrugs Travis."

"Bullshit," I huff. "Which one of your boys told you, but not me?"

He looks sheepishly towards the sky. "Maybe Wes or Gil...might have said something." Licking his lips, he leans closer in. "Man, she looks good. You would have thought all the stuff she fell into would have taken some of the shine."

"Well, that's what they say about black women. They don't crack and all," I whisper, while pretending to be looking at my cell.

"Hell, money helps, too. Shit, she lost it all, smoked, and partied away whatever her managers didn't steal."

"It be your own people, huh?" I comment, as we gossip like two bitches.

"Well?"

"Well, what?" I ask, as if I don't know what Travis is pressing to know.

He narrows his gaze at me. "You know damn well what I want to know."

"Lord man, Austin sent her here to learn to ride."

"Yeah, but what kind of beast?" he teases with a playful elbow to my ribs.

I fight back the sly smirk threatening to bloom across my face. "You can't expect me to run after a woman based on a childhood crush and late-night fantasies," I reply in what I hope is a convincing voice.

"Crush?!" he says a bit too loud, causing us both to steal a quick glance her way to ensure he wasn't heard. "Crush," he hisses low. "You were in love with that woman, even back then. Remember on your fifteenth birthday when Jessica tried to get fresh with you? You flat out told her you were taken," he begins to chuckle at my dumb youth. "Then, when Bradley asked you, you looked him straight in the face, serious as shit, to tell him that you were going to marry Naomi Henson."

This time, I can't stop the stream of laughter from erupting over the memory.

"Geesh," he moans. "It's good to see you laughing again. It's been too damn long," he says, becoming sober for a second, before returning back to his cheerful self. "Listen, it worked for the dude that played Aquaman, um, um...Jason Momoa," he recalls with a snap of his fingers. "He saw a chick on *The Cosby Show* when he was a kid, claimed her as his wife, then boom...he married Lisa Bonet. It can happen," he stresses.

Well, he and Austin seem to think so.

"At least she'll keep you from running tail," he mumbles under his breath, quickly. So, you've checked the barrels?" he asks, after clearing his throat.

"They're taking the bait, but not in the numbers we're used to," I grunt.

"So, I was right," sighs Travis. "We all know why, but we can't do anything about it," pausing, "Once I'm off the Reservation, I got no power."

"Still don't mean we're up shit creek with no paddle. I'm not letting those fuckers keep us from our festival," I promise.

"Hell no. The energy has been high for months for this. We got people traveling to attend. We're going to scare the fuck out of these pale faces with so many of us in one place," he jokes.

I nod. That also means a coming storm. Never fails for someone to be caught up in made-up bullshit to cause tension.

"Speaking of that, I'm doing things differently this year," I announce.

Understanding my meaning, Travis' grin stretches from ear to ear.

"Are you saying what I think you're saying? Are you actually bringing it back?" he asks loud enough to get Naomi's attention.

"I'm thinking that maybe it would be a good idea to-"

Giddy, due to what I was about to say, Travis bear hugs me.

"This is going to be one to remember," he shouts. "Just wait till...this means you're sticking around, then."

He doesn't give me a chance to answer.

"We'll all work to get shit together, okay?" talking more to himself than me, he glances out over the land. "Security and the set up will be on point. Trust me. Thank you," he sighs, as he claps his hands. "I'm going to head back." Pausing, he shifts his weight. "Um, I'm sure you know, but they're back."

Instantly my mood changes.

"I'm aware. Is there a problem?" I growl.

"With them, there's always a problem. Just waiting to see which way the shit is going to blow. I know I'm not Bradley, but I'm gonna say what he would have said...don't you think it's about time, son?"

A crooked smile hangs from my lips.

"You just make sure to turn a deaf ear when the time comes," I warn, slowly.

For a second, I see the fear in Travis' beady eyes. My statement is a pre-curser to the war that they have been waiting for but prayed to not get caught up in. Funny how he's ridden my ass for the last two years to stand up, do something, nip shit...and now that I'm to the point to do just that, he's fighting a desire to tell me to show restraint.

"You watch yourself," I plead.

We both know when I strike, it will be those close to me that will bear a target until I finish things.

"I'll be by in a few days, hopefully for a good update," he adds with a wink, before climbing on his ATV to speed off for the tree line.

I won't lie. All the talk about the wrinkle bitch of a mother and her greedy ass kids has me in a foul mood. Glancing over towards the shady tree line where I left Naomi, I'm not ready to pick up whatever I was doing. Instead, I choose to inspect the framework of the newly constructed sweat lodge. She appears to be fooling around with the horse at the moment to not even notice me.

Then again, I bet she sees me, just as much as I can't overlook her presence. It's a battle just to stay away. I want to be in her face, hear her voice, watch her eyes dilate due to my flirting that she pretends not to like is all I want to do. The fact that I'm so hell-bent on teasing her, to get under her skin...shit maybe even get between her legs if I'm lucky is a mounting temptation. It's like a schoolyard romance with the back and forth that will eventually end with us hutching and me getting my fingers wet behind the gym.

I don't fight the urge too long. The heat and not wanting her to do something to piss the mare off encourages me to settle my thoughts in regards to my family. I canter up to tower over her, still standing on the ground.

"I needed to give my ass a rest," she admits with a grunt. "The saddle hurts like hell."

My gaze follows her hand that rubs her upper, inner thigh dangerously close to her pussy. My silence must have given her cause to check on me.

"Why do I give you more fuel for the fire?" she groans.

"Why does the fact that I find you funny, sexy, and fuckable bother you?"

She pauses in mid mount to crush the grass under her foot.

"Have we ever met?"

I narrow my eyes, knowing where she was going with her question.

"No, I didn't think so. Yeah, you've met me in the many *roles* I have played, but you don't know *me*," she stresses to drive home her point.

With a frown, she cuts me with her eyes, traveling from my head to the tips of my leather, steel-toed boots, before mounting the mare.

"I don't have time for games. I have people that have put their money, trust, and time in me that I have to worry about. I got something to prove, and I can't fail. I'll be more than happy to gift you a copy of one of my skin flicks you can use a sock puppet too. Beyond that, all I want from you is training...of the horse," she adds to make things crystal clear.

I don't respond. All I do is pin Naomi with my hard gaze. Finally, I shift in the saddle.

"As you desire, Ms. Henson," I answer with a strained smile.

NAOMI

The nerve of this man. Oh, I can tell he's pissed. Can you believe he's mad at me because I refuse to let him dive in and beat *my* guts? Just fucking, wow. It would be a beating too. I can tell by the way he walks that he would fuck up my newly christened virgin coochie of three years sex free.

Jesus, *three* years?!

Maybe I should- NO! I shout mentally to the hoe raising her head to beg me to take another look of Zahn to consider all the many sweaty possibilities. I was completely in the right to put my foot down, I reassure myself. Then why is the newfound silence between us annoying me?

"So, because I'm not willing to give it up to you, you're going to turn all cold?" I say, suddenly. "That's a real bitch move, Zahn," I tsk dramatically.

From the corner of my eye, I watch his eyebrow reach for the sky.

"I don't want to say something that will have you clutching your pearls before running for your car."

"What car? If I had one, I think I would have folded day one," I chuckle. "And surely you can hold a conversation without coating every word in sex?"

"Coating in sex," he whispers in a groan. "Hey, your words, not mine," he exclaims with a wicked grin and his hands up in surrender.

"God man, are you that hard up?"

It takes me a second to realize that I'm riding alone. Not having learned how to turn the horse around, I command her to stop so I can physically do the action. Zahn is glaring at me as if I just committed a sin.

"All jokes aside, Naomi...I'll be honest with you."

A frown creases my forehead, as I wait to see what's behind the hard expression on his handsome face.

"Of course, I know who you are. Yes, I fantasized to you in my youth. No, I don't know you beyond your roles, and the gossip said about you. If half of what they say is true about your fall from grace, you've been through hell. From what you've heard, I wanted to be miles away from here and all the other bullshit brewing...but after realizing who you were...my dumb ass chose to stay. Listen to me closely. In spite of the fact that you are gorgeous, if there wasn't something else subconsciously drawing me to you, I wouldn't give your ass a second glance. Young pussy, old pussy, tight and so lose I can drive my pickup truck through it is thrown at me every day, so I'm not a man that chases a nut. I will tease you. I'm going to push your buttons. I'm going to say shit that will make you mad. I'm going to train you in a fashion that will make your panties wet...all in hopes that maybe, you might be willing-"

"Willing?" I repeat.

"Willing," he repeats, a bit slower on a whisper. "to explore."

Tilting my head, "How old are you, Zahn?"

"48...old enough that I don't play games, and to know what I want when I see it."

I search his face for the lie, only to find none there. Thankfully, the ranch is up ahead. I'm at a loss for words after a declaration like the one he just gave. How the hell does a person follow up after that? Absolutely relentless, to the point, with no chaser, is what he just did. Never has a man been so upfront and raw. Usually, it was drinks, dining, and promises of what would never be, and blowing smoke up my ass to get me in the sack. Instead, he dealt me a cut down by saying that I wasn't all that. To be honest, I'm thrown off balance. I don't know how I feel about being wooed in such a way.

Lost in my own thoughts, it takes him cursing under his voice to get me to acknowledge the cars parked in the front of his house. Without another warning, he kicks the stallion into running mode. I marvel at the sight of the hooves digging and dislodging the earth at the speed.

"Well, hi ho silver," I grumble.

Not willing to do the same, I let old Brook take her time to bring me to the front door.

"Problem?"

Rivers holds the door open for me. As I pass under the threshold, she answers.

"There's always a problem when a house is infested with rodents, but I got the right poison."

Yep, this woman is a real O.G.

CHAPTER SIX

ZAHN

My eyes survey my unwanted guest. I notice that there's more of them since the last mounted attack that was forged four months ago. Seated in the center is the woman that hated me to call her mother. I still did it, though. Even to this day, I would toss the word out to throw salt in the wound. Amazing how looks can be so deceiving. If a person didn't know her, Abby could pass as a breathtaking woman. Thankfully, I knew that her beauty was only skin deep.

Moving on to the other cast of characters in this train wreck. I glance over towards the back of my office. I'm not shocked to see that my adoptive sister went out of her way to ensure I get an eye full of the best body money can buy. I must admit that Jonelle's change from the limp blonde hair she was born with to the black shade does wonders for her complexion. Her blue eyes dazzle at my slightest attention.

I roll my eyes before nodding towards my adoptive brother. He's the only one that I pity. Jay was never good enough for neither of my parents. His lack of desire to farm and run the ranch didn't endear him to our father, while his feminine nature was an embarrassment to our mother. Poor Abby. The shit that was flung her way because she gave birth to the only male in years in her family line, only for him to be a closet gay.

Then there's Coby. The white-faced, son of a bitch, picked to represent the motherfucking farmers wanting my land. The other man sweating under my hard gaze, I don't know.

"I have things to do," I remark, kicking shit off.

"I can't say I have any love lost banning those thieves from my land," scowls Abby.

"God, yes. We don't need them godless fuckers messing with our daughters," growls Coby.

"Don't you mean your wives," I smirk. "How is Misty? I hope she got that mole on her back examined."

My smile deepens at the reddening of his face.

"Since you used the word, *my*...I can assume this is another try to take what's mine," I direct at Abby.

The slow aging bitch grins, while cutting her eyes at the man I've yet to be introduced to. Like handing a rabid dog a bone, his hand trembles as he lays an envelope on my polished walnut desk.

With a sigh, I scoop it up to remove the contents. A deep frown creases my forehead as I scan a few paragraphs.

"What the hell is this bullshit?" I question, tossing the crisp papers back onto the desktop.

"*This*," Coby taps the top page, "voids your claim."

"Is that so?"

Smuggly, Coby motions for the strange man to speak.

"I'm sorry to be meeting you on such an occasion...Sir, but it seems that the ranch, lands, and all the contents therein actually doesn't belong to the family or in this case...one man because of your ancestor, um Mr. Ewing senior...your *grand*father entered into an agreement with his fellow local farmers."

Slowly, I lock my hands behind my head while I lean back in my leather chair.

"And you mean for me to believe that not only did this all come to light after *all* of these years, but somehow, in a distant universe this...um, boys club, equals to my father's will wasn't worth the paper it was written on?" I inquire.

"It appears so," the lawyer replies on behalf of the rest that remain silent.

"I don't know you, man, but since you hitched your wagon to these fucks, you get the same, suck my dick, as them," I remark with a jerk of my head. "Get the hell out."

"Whatever, when the courts deliver the paperwork, it will be you getting out," shrugs Coby.

Placing my elbows on my desk, I pin the man with my gaze. "You and your boys must really like the smell of fish, by the way, ya'll are up her skirt," I finish with pointing my finger at Abby.

Her hand goes in the air to shut Coby up. "It was all a matter of time before your luck ran out."

"It will never stand."

She shrugs. "That's not what the local justice says," she responds smoothly.

I chuckle. "He finally named his price, huh?"

"Well, re-elections cost."

You could hear a mouse piss on cotton. The silence is just that thick in the room.

"I gotta know, is it the need for money?" I ask, although I know the answer.

"I have enough to do me right," Abby admits. "No, I can't stand your brown-skinned ass having all of this," she answers with a wide sweep of her ringed hand. "And I damn sure won't have you willing it over to the rest of them wild ginnies on the Reservation."

I nod. I take my time looking into each one of their faces. "This is your march, your last ride, your last time vexing mine with your bullshit attempts to get what's mine. I got no more cheeks to turn. See, you and your ole' boys got it all wrong in believing that *you* run shit. You are just visitors in *my* county...*allowed* to make a living on *my* people's land. Once I smack this down, and I will...if I see you again, if I smell your scent on the wind, I'm going to crush you into dust under my boot."

Unfazed as I knew the queen bitch would be, Abby gets to her feet. Shoulders back, spine ramrod straight, she pulls herself a few inches higher in her attempt to look down on me.

"Bradley did you a major disservice in making you believe you were our equal."

Tossing back my head, laughter that does nothing to soften my hard stare rings out. I catch Abby's slight bustling, before she heads for the door. The lawyer is skittish when he drops another set of legal documents on the table.

"I'm sorry for-"

I hold my hand up to stop the man caught in the middle of a long-ranging war. He nods. Getting to my feet, I head out into the hall.

NAOMI

"Fucking bitch."

I cut my gaze at Rivers. I angle my body to the side, upon hearing her hiss to watch the parade of unwanted guests, making their way for the front door.

"Is that his family?"

I was so caught up in being nosey, I hadn't seen Sali come up to join me.

"Yeah," I whisper. "You got any pillow talk?" I inquire.

"Didn't ask...but I will be, trust me," she answers out of the side of her mouth.

"Oh, shit! Rivers is stepping to his Mom," I point out in excitement.

In spite of the woman's spray-on tan, I notice her pale and blanch at the sight of the older woman. I narrow my eyes at her quick glance over her shoulder to ensure there's space between her and the others still lingering in the back of the large house. For some reason, Rivers takes great joy in letting his Mother get a good look at her.

"I didn't know you were still dragging your ass around her," Zahn's Mom starts things off.

Not annoyed, Rivers leans with her shoulder to the wall. "I'm like the old coo-coo clock that everyone tends to forget about with the passing of time...seeing and hearing so, *so* much."

The blonde woman shifts her weight on her pointy toe heels. My breath catches when she steps closer towards Rivers to speak.

"It would be a shame for such a relic of a clock to get busted."

Sali's fingers dig into my arm. "Did that lady just threaten Mrs. Rivers?" she whispers.

Not taking my eyes off the action, I try to shake my sister's death grip loose.

"Girl, hush." I'm straining to hear as it is.

"Busted," grunts Rivers. "What the fuck I care about that? I prefer busted to time rewinding around here."

Footsteps echoing get the ladies' attention. Even still, his Mother replies, "Does everyone feel the same way?"

The raised voices of the others drown out the two women still talking amongst themselves. My eyes dart further down the hallway. Something is going on between Zahn and the woman that must be his sister. By the deadpan expression on his face, whatever being said isn't going over too well with him. Suddenly, I cut back to the two older women to lock gazes with his mother. If I hadn't been hardened by the exclusion and racism of Hollywood, I might have shrunken back from the woman's glare. Instead, I meet her head-on, not blinking. Like all the others before, her reaction is predictable; surprise, fear, then anger that a person of color dares to challenge her as her equal.

"Jesus," she fumes. "The help around her just keeps getting darker and darker," she spits while making a trail for the front door.

This isn't my fight. I don't have a damn thing to do with this shit, I school myself.

But you can't let the bitch off like that, the voice in my mind commands.

The change in my persona comes naturally, as I slip into a role to shield and protect myself.

"Sweetheart, I can see you have unwanted guests. I'll be upstairs," pausing for dramatic effect now that all eyes were on me, I nonchalantly brush my stomach. "My nausea seems to always pass after lunch, so we can do whatever then."

I wait till I reach the third step to sway slightly. I don't have to glance over my shoulder to witness the looks of shock, worry, and confusion. A male clears his throat.

"This dry heat isn't for everybody," he comments.

Now, the baritone that speaks next I know. "That's the least of her problems," chuckles Zahn.

"Who the fuck is she?" shouts a female.

"You sly son of a bitch," hisses his Mom. "I'll-"

"Get the fuck out," he growls. "*Now*," he thunders.

He isn't talking to me, but I move my ass up the remaining stairs and down the hall as if he is. I can make out the sound of the soles of shoes doing the same thing. I slam my door just in time to hear Rivers' stream of curses.

ZAHN

I can't take my eyes off the stairs Naomi disappeared up. Nothing, not even Rivers bitching at me can remove the wicked grin from my face.

"See, she's only been here for a few days, and she has more fight than you," huffs Rivers. "Are you fucking listening to me? Don't try to tune me out," she snarls, followed with a punch that bounces off my arm muscles.

"Make sure she eats," I order while heading for the door.

"Where you going?"

"To handle things."

Rivers visibly stiffens. "I'll make sure that you do," she mumbles.

I got no time for her riddles. I'm just as tired and ready to finish this goddamn bullshit as the rest of them are. I don't need to be told what to do. Shit, I've spent days on end planning how I would fuck my family and the farmers sucking their dick. I have no more fucks for these people. I'm not aiming to shake the boat. I'm planning to blow the shit up.

I smile at the sight. For the last 2 years, I've been collecting these sacks of seed. Once I realized that I had been spending a fortune for a seed that wouldn't produce a crop no matter how fertile the soil, I didn't toss it. Quickly, I count the sacks. Happy with the number, I move along to find who are going to be my partners in crime. I know I don't have to prime the pump where Wes, Gil, or Graham is concerned. I'm not even done with telling my plan and they are already on board.

"You really mean business, huh?"

"I don't want them to have a blade of grass to wipe their asses with," I reply.

Graham lowers his head to kick at the dirt.

"You know we're good as dead if we're caught. They'll soon as kill you, Zahn, then call the law," he warns, slowly.

"Then we won't get caught. You know how to move in the shadows, and let my hands be the only one seen," I order.

The three brothers I see as my own fall silent.

"Look, we all know that things can't go on as they have been...and we're always squeezing your balls about it, but-"

"Then let me finish it," I remark, cutting Wes off. "Until they have the papers to this place, I'm free to move. They won't risk my will being enforced out of fear that it all goes back to the Reservation."

"What?! It's not all going to your baby?"

It takes me a second to catch on to the joke. I can't stop my chuckle.

"For the record, she has my vote."

Gil's comment gives me a reason to pause.

"She's here to train for a role...they both are," I add, as I shift my gaze towards Graham. "They aren't staying," I stress.

His brothers won't look in his direction. No doubt they wanted to tell him the same thing. I just have the balls to say it. Graham is the nicest bastard around. Too nice when it came to love, which is why he struck out with the women. His love for books, jazz, and other shit was a loss on many of the chicks. The females were after his dick, not his heart, which he longed to give away.

"But you want her, don't you?"

Now, I could play dumb at this point, but I won't.

"I do, but that won't change the fact that this isn't her world, her land, her people. I'll enjoy getting my dick wet and her time, but my heart is my own."

"If that's what you want to believe."

I narrow my eyes at Graham. He has a way of speaking shit upon people. I'll be a pissed off motherfucker if that's what he's just done to me. He can fall in love with hopes of tying Naomi's sister down, but not me. Things moaned and grunted should stay between the sheets, not to be taken seriously.

"The junior hunt is next week, the festival following, I want shit done," I growl before I leave.

I'll let Graham play the damn fool. I have shit to get done from dealing with my family, to getting things ready for the festival, to the daily running of the ranch, to yes, Naomi. I don't even notice the smile tugging on the corner of my mouth till it's full bloom. Annoyed, I instantly remove it for a frown.

"Shit," I hiss.

Instead of going to the barn, I make a beeline for my pick up. Distance is the only thing that will keep me from seeking out that damn woman.

"I haven't even stabbed it, and I'm hooked," I grunt while slamming the truck door.

By the time I drive the 40 miles into town, I'm focused. It's time to put into action the plan I've been holding onto for the last six years. A few of the players have retired to be replaced with new faces. No matter, though. The new characters are just as corrupt as the old ones. The game is still the same. If it's one thing Bradley taught me is how to bluff, when to apply pressure, and most of all, how to crush your opponent, to win. There will be no fairness, no going high.

Funny how my presence in town is received. Money, lots of money, is truly king. Yeah, I know that many of the smiles, waves, and shouts of my name are fake. The majority of the people doing so would spit in my face if I didn't hold in my hands all I do. Then, there are the women openly flirting as I walk through the doors of the courthouse. With a knowing smirk, I tip my wide brim hat.

As a child, I always marveled when Bradley would march right in on the judge or the mayor to demand them to do as he commanded. In my eyes, he was a superhero and everyone must have known it, too, because the people actually did as he ordered.

"Mr. Ewings."

The poor young girl looks as if she just saw a ghost.

"Carol, right?"

Lord, I pray she doesn't faint.

"Y-yes," she laughs nervously, while stumbling to her feet. "You remember my name," she blushes.

I tilt my head, as I let my eyes roam just enough to give her the sense that I'm sizing her up.

"Of course, I would remember you."

Yeah, cuz I called the office not 20 minutes ago, and you told me when you answered the phone. I bet if I sniffed, I could smell the cum wetting her cotton panties.

"Is the Judge in?"

She takes time to lick her thin lips. "Oh, yeah, but, um…he's on a call."

"Nothing that will take all day, I hope?"

Stealing a glance at the closed door, she leans in closer than what's needed to answer.

"If you must know, it's about you," she whispers.

I have to school my expression. I wasn't expecting her to tell all the business so easily. After lunch, a cheap coffee, maybe kissing and cumming around my fingers up against a wall, but not without getting something first. You got to love the empty-headedness of the younger generation.

"Me? I haven't been home long enough to break the law," I chuckle.

"Well, Mr. Coby was here. Then the calls started, so you got up somebody's ass."

Dramatically, I sigh. "I just can't catch a break…and after all, I do for this town," I shake my head, sadly.

Carol's lips form into a pout. She reaches over to place her palm on my arm either to comfort or to use it as an excuse for contact.

"I know. It's sickening how *some* people talk. Whenever I hear that bullshit, I'm quick to shut them down," she promises.

Her comment is rewarded with a beaming smile on my face that causes her to gasp. Yes, I'm that bastard. I'm going to use her ass, and not in the way she's hoping. I hold her gaze while I remove her hand to slowly bring it to my lips. I brush her knuckles.

"You make an old man feel good," I whisper.

Hoping to hear a bit of his convo, I swing Judge Shine's door open. No luck. With a shit-eating grin, he slowly hangs up on the female voice cursing through the line. My guess, it's Abby.

"Come, sit your ass down," he offers with a sweep of his hand.

He's happier than a tick. No doubt he's counting the dollar signs in his mind from the bidding war he thinks is going to ensure to get him to my side. I toss my hat into the hard leather chair next to the one I take in front of his desk.

"If you grin wider, you'll have a crack bigger than your ass splitting your ugly mug," I smile.

Gleefully, he tosses back his head. His face turning flush, making him look like a fat radish.

"Well, at least I am. I can't say the same about some people," he remarks while tapping his office phone. "Are you here to give your side of the story?"

"You mean to clear up the lies?" I retort.

"Oh, the truth? Well, that's open to interpretation. Congrats on your new development in all of this."

"It's too soon for fan fair."

"Hum, yes…anything can happen with pregnancy. It would be wiser to have a concrete decision…just in case," he nods with a mock expression of seriousness. "There's no need for you to tell me how you would *like* things to go. I'm trying to see if I can?"

I pin the man with my hard gaze.

"Because their case is so strong?" I ask, slowly for clarification.

"Well, yes," he sighs. "It seems Bradley's father wasn't as…soft hearted towards your people. He wanted his lands to stay with-"

"The white thieves that stole it," I interject, getting a bit gruff."

"I can't change history. I can only work in the now."

"But for a better deal?"

"Which is?" he presses.

I huff. "You actually think I'm going to put money in your pudgy ass hand? No, you're going to do what I want because I *told* you too."

Shocked silence is what happens to Judge Shine. This time, he goes red not of laughter, but anger.

"Fuck y-"

"And this is why you're going to watch your fucking mouth, you beetle shaped motherfucker."

Tapping the face of my cell, I hold up the phone to allow him to get a good look. From red to colorless, his jaw becomes unhinged. Out of fear, he lunges for my hand.

"Thought going around the world to fuck little boys was the way to go, huh?" I sneer. "How do you do that? Fuck boys the same age as your grandsons? Do you imagine their innocent faces while you-"

"SHUT UP! SHUT UP!"

"No, see, you don't get to order shit!"

He scrubs his palm down his face with a shaking hand.

CHAPTER SEVEN

NAOMI

The house is quiet when I finally decide to leave my room hours later. The empty dishes from the lunch Rivers brought up to me are balanced in my hand. I'm thankful that everyone seems to be off doing whatever. To be honest, I kept to my room to avoid the drama that was already simmering long before I touched down. It's drama that I really don't want to know. If I'm not aware, then I won't have a reason to care, which I find myself doing enough of already.

I mean, damn. You know how there's always two sides to a story; the person's version and then the truth? Well, I bet if I could examine the truth, it would line up with everything Zahn's told me about his family already. That bitch of an adoptive mother is foul. Why the hell would Zahn's father choose to bring him into a racist home? It's just fucking cruel. To have to live in a home where you're alone, unwanted, mistreated is...

I shake myself.

This has nothing to do with me. I'm not here for nothing more.

Placing the dishes on the countertop, I lean back to gather my thoughts. I have to get my shit together. The fact that I know he's crushing on me is messing with my head. The allure of having a man, an attractive one, one so different from the clowns

I'm used to, and one that I can tell is still carrying the wounds of his youth is creating a formula of both distraction and disaster.

The notion that because we both come from fucked up situations doesn't mean a thing. So, don't get it in my head. He would never, never understand me.

"Why do I even care? I've only known this man a day, day and a half? Lord," I grumble to myself.

So, why do I feel green around the gills as I make my way to find him? I hate it, not being in control. I hate the fear of wondering if I'm being seen as I really am; unconfident, scared, damaged. I hate the longing of wanting to tell my secrets to a man that talks one helluva game, no doubt to get what every man in my life only wanted.

By the time I glimpse him, head down, reading papers behind a desk, I've worked myself into a state. Hiding in the hallway, I pat my pills in my front pocket. I place my hand in to finger the plastic top while I debate popping a pill before going in. Tossing my head back, I glare angrily at the ceiling over my reaction at the thought of being in the same room with him.

I'm 42, well-traveled, well worn, very experienced woman.

I search my mind for a role I can slip into but come up with nothing to suit. Or maybe, I don't want one. Chewing on my bottom lip, I inch closer to the door, take a deep breath, and force my fist to move towards the door frame to knock.

"So, you won the battle, huh?" he asks, still looking downward.

I would've thought without his piercing eyes on me, I would be more fluent in speech, but I was wrong. With his head bowed, it gives my eyes freedom to stare, and me time to lust. I never realized till now how much a man's working hand turned me on. I was never one for soft anything. Soft hands, soft handshake, or a soft dick...and I'm sure Zahn is incapable of giving me either. The thick, raised veins in his hands that ran along his arms are proof of the years of hard work and labor he's put in.

"Well," I start, only to have to pause to clear my throat. "you said 5'o clock," I manage to get out of a mouth that's gone dry.

He nods his head a few times, yet still has me holding my breath, waiting. I feel like a schoolgirl waiting for a hot teacher to give me his attention. I fight the urge to wring my hands. Unable to stay rooted, I turn to leave. I can already feel a pout coming on for not being able to spend more time with him. Shit! What the hell is wrong with me?

"You're busy so, we can skip it."

"Why did you say what you said earlier? The hinting off?"

I twirl back to be gut-punched by the force of his eyes. I work my mouth in hopes of giving him a quick answer, but my vocal cords and brain are making a fool out of me.

"You didn't have to do that," he states, standing.

"I know," I reply in a rush. "I'm sorry if it's going to bring the roof down on you," I tease.

"The rafters been exposed long before you. Trust me," he smirks. "You just gave them something to keep them up at night.

Don't let his smile fool you. He's studying you.

"Shit, that old bitch needs all the sleep she can get," I huff.

He chuckles while coming from behind the desk. I can't move. Then again, why the hell would I want to? He suddenly looks all boyish with the way he slides the hands I've caught myself thinking about into his back pockets.

"Thank you."

Deep, raspy, and warm. That's the only way to describe the sound of Zahn's voice.

I shake my head. "I overstepped by getting involved. I spoke before I even knew what I was doing. She caught me wrong."

"I think the terms are rude and racist."

In spite of all of the warnings and inner coaching, I find myself doing shit that will only bring me closer to this man.

"So, that's her? Your adoptive mother?"

All he does is nod.

"Man, I'm sorry," I grumble. "As a child, you expect love from the person you call Mom...and to realize you'll never have it, it's a tough blow."

Pull back. You're showing too much.

"Um, so...yeah," I stumble, as I take a step back to put more space in between.

His hand grabs mine to slowly bring me back.

"You would make a great Mom."

His words are like a bucket of icy cold water. The spell has been broken. I can see he knows it too by the deep frown on his brow in his attempt to figure out why I've gone rigid.

"Wrong," I say sternly. "your work is calling," I point out to end the conversation.

Once again, I try to stroll out. Once again, he jerks me back.

"What did I do wrong? Why what I said piss you off?" he demands to know.

He isn't easing up on his grip.

"Why I'm pissed is because I think you're confusing me with my past roles. It's called *acting* for a reason, Zahn. Make-believe, pretend, and so fucking far from the truth, it can *never* be a reality."

"I'm sorry," he whispers.

How can words spoken so softly still be hard enough to cut? Sour is what I am at the sight of pity in his eyes. Another person to feel sorry for poor me. Another person to handle me with kid gloves, to tsk under their breath at the sight of my brokenness.

With a jerk that surprises him, I free myself. I should be the one pitying him and his crappy upbringing. His own Mom gave him the hell up. What right does he have to stare at me like this…? The desire to remove myself from the spotlight has me wanting to inflict pain. Instead, I clam up to keep from giving in. Still, in my rational mind, I know I shouldn't punish him for something he has no idea about, nor should I give him a verbal bashing for trying to show me a bit of kindness, no matter his motive. Even still, I need to leave before I flip the switch.

"Thank you," I hiss through a forced smile.

This time, Zahn's smart enough to let me go.

ZAHN

It took a complete day for the strange cloud and awkwardness between us to disappear. By day two, we stopped treating each other with kid gloves, and she was finally able to look me in the face. Now on day three, we're yelling at each other as if nothing had happened. Every day, I tell myself that Naomi is making progress…only for her to backslide.

"Loosen up," I shout, while she trots the horse around me.

"I am," she snaps back.

I wonder why I'm taking a beating from the blistering sun above. Although it's a cool day, being in the direct rays of the sun is a bitch. Frustrated, I snatch my hat from my head.

"You're riding constipated."

"Yeah, cuz you're up my ass," she shouts.

I grind my teeth.

"Do you know how to ride dick? Well, do you?" I press when she doesn't answer.

I place my fingers in my mouth. A high whistle echoes. Naomi is no longer in control, as the mare comes to stand in front of me.

"Have you ever fucked on top?"

"Yes," she hisses, at last.

"Show me your hip work?" I order, as I walk to the side of the horse.

"The heat's messing with you," she frowns.

"No, move your hips. Come on," I added firmly.

"I'm not going to-"

"I swear if you don't-"

"Fine!" she sneers. Stealing a quick glance around, Naomi rocks her hips a few quick times.

"Jesus, a man would do better whacking his monkey. What the fuck was that?" I ask while I mimic her actions.

"Should I have twerked?" she mocks, annoyed.

"Don't turn all bitch on me," I warn. "It's hot as hell, and I got shit to do."

"Then take your ass on and do it then, instead of yelling at me as if I'm not trying," she spits.

Lowering my head, I place my hat back on. I take a deep breath. When I look back up, I hope my expression is hiding my mounting anger.

"Come ride me."

Expressionless, she stares down into my face.

"You heard right, come on," I say at the sight of her opening her mouth to speak. "Clothes on, so no worries other than my sure to be hard on, which I'm willing to deal with later to get you over this hurdle."

I have no time to continue to coax her. I reach up and drag her out of the saddle. In one movement, we both fall to the ground. She keeps taking peeks toward the house in the distance. Quickly, I shake her.

"Me, I'm all you should be focusing on. Now, open your legs."

My hands grip her hips to lift her in the air. Her legs open to straddle me. Another adjustment places her on my already firm dick.

"Um," she coughs to hide a moan. She's completely unsure of my methods.

"Now, make me cum," I order.

I know she's not going to move her stiff body. Slowly, I begin to buck under her, setting the tempo.

"Ride me, Naomi," I beg.

My hands tighten on her hips to force her to move. It's not long before she's swaying on her own. Our jeans do nothing to hide the heat radiating from her pussy. No longer giving a damn about the purpose of this exercise, I already know I'm going to press for more. Open palm on her back, I push her forward, towards me. She refuses by planting her palms flat on my chest, to remain upright. I pin her with my narrowed gaze. I can read her fear and fight in the depths of her brown eyes. Yet, I also can see a glimmer of something else; lust and intrigue.

I wonder if she notices the way her fingertips are brushing my chest to test the muscles under them.

"Use your thighs. Flex them to tell me what you want. Do you want me to move slow," I change the pace, "Want it hard?" With my hands on her hips, I force her down as I grind my hips hard against her. Leaning up onto my ass, "Or fast? It's all communicated in your thighs...and your hips flow with the rhythm," I explain.

Reaching back, I caress and massage her ass. Her parted lips are mere inches from mine. So damn close. I debate if I should. Hell, we're humping for all to see. Why the hell not go in for a kiss?

NAOMI

What the hell happened? Shit, I know what happened. I'll play shocked later, but what's happening is exactly what I've been dreaming of. No, my dreams don't come close to what I'm actually experiencing. Zahn isn't a slow burn. He's a goddamn tsunami. Bee stung lips fuse with mine. I can't even get it together long enough to prove to him that I'm a good kisser. He invades my mouth to dominate me.

I should stop. I-I need to get up, and, an-

Yet, my arms rise to lock around his neck, as I scoot even closer. Suddenly, the hot and heavy becomes something different. Zahn changes the mood again. His mouth moves over mine, as he deepens the kiss. His hands take control of my hips to slow them down. I'm starting to gain control of my senses. I'm ready to join the game.

My acting is great. My dick game is amazing, or so I was praised years ago. Then again, those were the same liars that promised to love me. Back in the day, I brought to the table confidence and years of practice that I should be ashamed of. However, I find myself trapped in my head, instead of being in the moment. I sway my hips to the tempo. I focus and breathe deeply of his scent of sweat and earth. Making Zahn happy is easy. Shit, with enough pumps, any man can be satisfied. The true test of a good lover is if he can satisfy his woman? I thought I had a few amazing rumps in my past. They made me tingle, my pussy got wet, yet I don't think I ever really had a-

I'm snatched from my inner thoughts at the feel of his hands needling my ass. There's nothing hidden between us. The size of his dick is no longer speculation. My fingers itch to gravitate downward to trace the length and width. Even still, I have enough information to calculate and conjure up an image of his cock that's thicker than it is long. He's still packing an impressive 8 inches with one helluva wide girth, though.

We can't seem to get close enough. I want to laugh at the fact that we're both sitting in the dirt, in the hot sun, and anyone could catch us making out like two school kids.

"Damn, you're an ego crusher," he breathes into my mouth.

"What are we doing?" I chuckle nervously.

"I'm trying to show you I'm the one that's going to blow your back out."

I can't contain my laughter. It's the way he said it, not the promise. His arms snake around my waist to hold me while tremors rack my body. When I calm down, I crack my eyes to find his handsome face dark with an emotion that causes me to swallow the last remnants of glee.

"I'm sorry," I mumble, while trying to dislodge myself from his hold.

"No," he states, locking me in a vice-like grip.

I flinch at the sight of his hand, moving towards my face. In that one reaction, I've communicated so much, and I know he didn't miss it.

"Never lose that, Naomi," he smiles. Touching his hand to my cheek, he caresses it. "That's the first time you've laughed. Let yourself go...it's really beautiful to see."

All I can do is blink because I've lost my ability to speak again with this man. Is he serious? I mean, it seems so cheesy coming from a past like mine. Is what could be a line in a movie really happening to me? I can't contemplate because, at the moment, Zahn's face, his lips are moving across the bit of space between us for another kiss.

What would happen if I just...let...go?

The brush of his lips to mine is light, barely a hair's breath, but the heat in the act is electrifying. So much that my heart is beating to break through my chest. I'm panting, but not for the reasons I should be.

Slowly, he pulls away. Our eyes lock. He's calculating. Yeah, he's probably realizing just how fucked up and ruined I am. Like second nature, I plaster a winning smile on my face in hopes that it's enough to dazzle Zahn so that he doesn't truly see. Yet, his gaze never leaves my brown eyes.

How will this play out? I worry that the cloud of awkwardness that finally had lifted maybe coming back. I don't want that either.

"No more training for today."

His declaration causes my heart to sink and accelerate at the same time. It takes everything in me not to show my disappointment on my face. I wish I knew what to do with myself once Zahn removes me from his firm body. My movements are choppy. I try to play it off by beating the dirt and dust from my pants. In doing so, I can hide my face for a few more moments.

Why isn't he going? He's just standing there, watching me.

"I'm not rejecting you."

I want to deny that's exactly what I was thinking, but I can't.

"I have work to do for the hunt. Come with."

Jesus, I'm like a puppy...secretly all giddy to be in his orbit.

"I'm sure I'm ready to do better after such a riveting demonstration," I tease.

Sticking out my tongue, I rock my hips while in the saddle. Zahn moans and winks.

"I'll be damned," I mumble in awe.

It worked. It actually worked. It's like night and day. With a light squeeze of my thighs, the mare switches from walk to a trot. In utter amazement, I glance back at Zahn. He leaps on his own horse.

"Ready for a run?"

With a nod, I hand over the reins to him. There's no way I'm going to take off running in the woods. He makes a sound, and the horses leap into action. I thought my grip on the saddle horn was tight. The jerking into motion damn near causes me to fall backwards to the ground. The landscape whizzes by in a rush. The pounding of the earth under the horse's hooves is loud and scary-ass hell. So, why the hell am I laughing like a crazy woman? Why am I experiencing a sense of freedom unlike any other? Why do I trust this man to lead me through the woods at such a neck-breaking pace?

My eyes dart over to him. His blue-black braids are flapping in the wind behind him. And I catch myself doing what I accused Sali of doing. Could Zahn Ewings be the embodiment of the men written in those Native American romances after all?

I shake the outrageous thought from my mind. It's funny how not long ago, a tree was just a tree. However, I'm able to make out certain areas to figure out where we're headed.

"Fucking hell."

Wide eyed, I look around the space with the exposed dome shape building he took me to before. I frown. Nothing seems to have changed from the last time.

A string of curses echoes through the clearing as he fishes his cell from his back pocket. Wisely, I stay silent.

ZAHN

"Have you been out here?"

"Whatcha talking about? No, I haven't. Tsoise's boys signed up for first shift at site. They didn't start work?"

"If they did, I wouldn't be calling," I shout through the phone at Travis.

I have to pull the cell away from my ears to keep from going deaf. I gaze out over the land the size of three football fields in disgust. Today was supposed to be the beginning of getting shit ready for the festival. We needed all the time allotted to pull this off. I swear, at times, I think my own people are against me. One second they claim to be on board and ready to help. Then in their next breath, they complain about the amount of work and refuse to pitch in. Many want the benefits, but only if it's given without any output.

"Listen, I'm on my way to stop Lucy from putting a hole in her son's ass. I can't come till much later, but I can send up a call to get-"

"No worries," I state, cutting him off. "I'll get stuff done."

"Lord, man, you can't do all that needs to happen. You need help," he stresses.

"Apparently not...nobody else thinks so."

Annoyed, I hang up. My bones suddenly feel weary, as I conjure up the long list of shit that should have been done by now and the amount of time that's left. All I can do is stand and stare at the bare bones of the sweat lodge.

"I can help."

The offer, so unheard of to me, pulls me out of the rivers of depression. I had forgotten Naomi was even here. I muster up a tired smirk.

"Nah, I got it."

Old nature kicks in. Reaching into my saddlebag, I remove a pair of thick, yellow suede working gloves. Walking her way, she sidesteps to get out of my path for the lodge. On the far side of the structure, under a tarp, is a pile of hides.

"You know I can help with all of this."

I stop in mid bend to glance over my shoulder to find her with her hands on her hips.

"I'm out here...and what else am I going to do?" she sasses.

Still not too convinced, I arch an eyebrow in the way of asking her if she's really sure.

"Just show me what to do?" she presses with an outstretched hand for me to pass her a covering.

"Okay," I smile, finally giving in.

Tugging off the gloves, I hand them over to her. After a quick instructional, a few trials and errors, we create a system.

"This for the hunt?"

Pausing, I stand to wipe the sweat from my brow. In spite of the cooler weather, the labor is still kicking our asses.

"No, the younger ones aren't allowed in the lodge. They have to be seen as adults first."

"And that's what the hunt is, right? Like a passage into manhood?"

"Shit, if that was all it took," I grumble.

"You're mad, aren't you?" she asks.

Stopping, I stand to toss my head back. Eyes closed, I exhale, slowly. I find myself telling Naomi what I've never fully expressed to anyone.

"Mad, really frustrated, disappointed," I list out.

"Then don't do it. Fuck it. Once you quit, people will-"

"Sit on their asses, and nothing will get done," I reply. Dropping my head, I lock eyes with her. "I've tried that...my father did too, and people suffered." I shake my head, as I get back to work. "There are others that care."

"Then why aren't they here?"

"Because they can't...and preserving the way is more important at the end of the day."

When her stream of questions ceases, I glance up to see why only to find her looking at me strangely.

I ignore what I see written on her face.

"This is the biggest gathering for the Tribe. People travel from all over, even from other countries to take part. Usually, I just host the activities, but this year," I say with a crazed chuckle, "I got it in my mind to do it the way my old man used to...with everyone camping out here," I remark with a nod of my head towards the open land. "Every year there's always something with the locals accusing a tribesmen of some shit. Hopefully, with everyone being here instead of the town or Reservation, it won't be any drama," I explain.

"How many you talking?"

"300…maybe 500."

"Sweet Jesus," she hisses in amazement.

"Yeah," I grin.

"Sounds exciting," she admits, as she ties another panel down to the lodge's frame.

"Me and a few others have been training this year's batch of boys for months. Teaching them how to track, camp, hunt with a bow…. for them to be able to put their skills to use is a sign that they are ready to be seen no longer as boys, but young men. They'll have 2 days to bring back a deer."

"They'll be going as a group, right?"

"No," I answer. "On their own."

This time Naomi gives me a stuck on stupid kinda look. I debate telling her about the highlight of this year's festival being the Sundance. I'm sure if I described the tradition that included self mutilation, she would really think I've lost it. I skip that to tell her about the other fun activities. She interrupts every now and then to ask a question, or maybe to let me know she's actually listening while she works.

"That's good for now," I announce after 2 hours of working.

I take note of the fact Naomi doesn't fight me to keep going. She can care less that the roof of the lodge is still uncovered. **Hell,** she beats me back to the horses.

"Can you ride?"

"Yeah," she assures me.

I don't care, though. I want to create a similar level of intimacy from before.

"You look ran over."

"Thank you, Zahn," she grunts.

Shit! My eagerness is fucking me up. The goal isn't to get her pissed, but to make her soften towards me.

"I didn't mean it like that. I mean, you look tired. I can't have you falling out of the saddle."

Good, I can see her considering my words. I take advantage to pluck her off her feet to sit her on my horse. Before she can object, I swing up behind her. I'm glad she can't see the wide grin on my face when she relaxes to lean back. My arm snakes around her waist to hold her tightly. My pace is slow. I don't want to rush this time together.

"Did you bring a few warmer pieces? We are going to have a few cooler days and colder nights."

"Um, no. I just assumed-"

"I have somethings you can borrow," I offer.

The thought of seeing her in my clothes excites the hell out of me. We fall silent. Why does this feel like a first date?

There's a weirdness brought on by the kiss…and the grinding added to it, too. I haven't felt so unsure around a woman in years. The myth that this shit gets easier with age is a lie. Honestly, it's a rush to both of my heads.

I shift, which causes her to fit even closer to me. I lick my dry lips as I search for something to talk about to break the silence.

"I remember my first hunt."

"I'm shocked you can remember that far back," she teases.

The rest of the ride is filled with me reliving the event with comical details. I can't get enough of her laughter. My heart flutters every time she gives over to a carefree mood. As much as I want to drag it out, the house materializes through the trees. Once again, we both fall quiet.

"Thank you for helping," I say when I dismount and pull her down from the horse.

I should release her. I should give her space. Yet, I don't, and she doesn't force me to do so, either. Instead, I read the uncertainty in her eyes. How the hell can she wonder if I'm interested? Or maybe I'm misreading the reason altogether.

"What are you thinking?"

It's a dumb question. Most people will tell you nothing, or straight out lie.

"Are you going to kiss me again?"

I go ramrod straight. Did I hear her, right? Well, I'm not going to ask her to repeat herself. I move cautiously, in case I'm wrong. Lowering my head slowly, I watch Naomi. I instantly notice the difference when our lips touch. This kiss isn't the same. She's communicating so much that I'm in overload when I pull back for air. From the look in her eyes, she felt it, too.

I'm so lost in it all that it only takes a gentle push on my chest to make me stumble back. In awe, I follow Naomi with my eyes as she walks away, only to turn back a few steps later.

"Since you have no problem giving advice, I'm going to drop a bit of wisdom on you. If you were to die today, the world would keep on turning, and the people you're stressing over will find a way without you. Leeches will feed till there is no more, but trust me...they won't die. They'll just latch on to another. There's only so much blood you got to give."

The entire time she spoke, she did so with a smile. Yet, her words hit like damn rocks.

CHAPTER EIGHT

NAOMI

THREE DAYS LATER...

"I should've not said anything."

I've been playing that on repeat for the last three days. Lip poked out, I toss the warn and marked up script on the bed. Rolling over onto my stomach, I sigh like a lovesick teeny bopper. Frustrated, I bury my head in my pillow.

"Everything was going so well, we kissed...and I had to drop some knowledge," I say in a deep, mocking voice. "Shit!" I scream, punching the pillow.

I fucked up. Nothing new, huh? Zahn packed up and disappeared. I had no right to tell him that he shouldn't be so ready to help others. I mean, these are his people, his tribe. All I was trying to do was tell him to put himself first. No, that's not entirely true.

Giving to those in need is good and all, but not to the point that home suffers. Then again, maybe that's why he never married. It's hard when there's so many in a relationship. My career was my main focus back in the day, and my love life suffered. Hell, shouldn't my career be the main focus, now?

"Ugh!" I yell.

Rolling out of bed, I attempt to shake off the lingering rejection.

"This is good," I tell myself.

I'M NOT HERE FOR ROMANCE. I SHOULDN'T HAVE EVER STARTED ANY OF THIS SILLINESS WITH THAT MAN. STICK TO THE DAMN PLAN.

I don't need to turn to see who knocked before entering. It's been an ongoing occurrence over the last three days. As if I needed more to make me realize how much I've fucked things up, Sali's taken it upon herself to lighten up my life with accounts of what's going on in hers.

"Girl, I got to tell you this."

I make sure to remove my face of any genuine emotions when I turn to give her my attention. Now, I have to pretend to listen. Shit, of course, I'm hanging on every damn word she's speaking regarding Graham. The man is amazing. His sex game is on point. I got to admit, I'm intrigued about the oral thing. I won't let on, but I've never had a man's mouth on me down there. I've sucked many dicks in my day, but as for any of them returning the favor, none ever did. Surely not the ones that I fucked while on the streets. Who wants to tongue fuck a crack head?

I'm holding my breath while wondering if Zahn is half the man as Graham? The thought only makes me want to see him even more.

"That's sounds...he did all of that?" I question, still a bit dumbfounded.

"Hand on the Bible," she promises. Beaming, sitting on the side of the bed, she swings her legs happily. "He's the total package. I swear," she sighs.

"Only downfall is he's here."

"That can change, though."

I roll my eyes. "Don't do this, sis. You can't make that man leave for pussy."

"What if I'm offering him more than that?"

Her question wipes the smirk from my face. Don't get me wrong. I'm happy if Sali's happy. I'm slapped with the knowledge I'm still leaning on her, depending on her in so many ways. It's a place that I've been fighting to get out of, and this is the reason why. Even still, where am I left with if she and Graham do take things further than carefree fucking?

"Come on...I can see your toes are curled, but you can't be that serious?" I chuckle as I try to make light of her feelings.

As soon as the words leave my mouth, I feel like shit. I'm not thinking about the fact that my sister has been kicked around and used by men. I don't consider that this love with Graham could be the real deal and her only real chance at love. Instead, I'm a petty bitch that's focused on my own interests.

I watch a bit of Sali's excitement ebb. I can visibly see her second questioning herself.

"You really want to try?"

She lifts her head. "I've never felt this way before. I know that sounds cheesy...and I know we're so different, but it's more than the sex. It's the way he makes me feel. It's the fact that he TRIES to understand me and not make me feel as if I have to shrink myself to make him feel like a man. I like how he talks. Even when he's putting me in my place, he does it in a way that I'm not mad."

"That's some amazing shit. Right there alone is reason enough," I mumble. "Hold on. If you and him can work it out, try to make it work," I say with a loud hand clap.

"Really? You don't think I'm jumping the gun?"

"I'm not talking signals because those can get crossed and nobody has time for that...but if he's TELLING you that he wants more," I pause to shrug, "Go for it," I finish in a rush.

Sali jumps to her tennis shoe feet with a shit-eating grin on her face. I can't stop the laughter at the sight of her dancing for the door.

"Thanks," she says in the open doorway, "You've always been so good at giving advice. Make sure to take some of it, too."

I open my mouth to call her back to explain what she meant, but I won't play dumb. I already know.

ZAHN

The noise from the blades powering down drowns out the ringing of my cell.

"Hello!" I shout. "Hold on a sec!" I yell as I widen my strides to put distance between me and the helicopter.

The name on the caller ID makes me chuckle.

"What the fuck you want?" I snap.

"I wanna know what you've done?"

Confused, I frown. Jerking the glass door open, I stay in the waiting room area.

"Can't be too much. I've been on the trail," I inform Austin.

"Shit, man, don't be fuckin things up," he explodes. "What about the Hunt and the fest?"

"Both are going on as planned. I had to check on the cattle drive," I explain. Tossing my bags in a nearby seat, I try to figure out what's up.

"Oh," he breathes, relaxing a bit. "Mag's boys have been up my ass for months. They'll have my balls if I told them it's been called off. Jesus, can you believe Manny and Craig are old enough for their first buck?"

"No," I laugh as I conjure up the images of the once pudgy boys running around my house on their visits.

Although Austin and Mag were proud of their heritage, it wasn't a fact that most in the world knew. The natural olive skin they got from their Lakota father was assumed by others to come from an Italian relative.

"I'll have a car to meet them at the airport," I promise. "Um, I heard from Rivers about Dani."

The line goes quiet as I know that it would.

'That's none of my business," he states.

"Not mine either, but that doesn't stop me from having an opinion."

"What did the old lady tell you?"

"That Dani's husband isn't letting her come to the festival," I answer.

"' YOU AREN'T GOING TO HOWL AT THE MOON LIKE A DAMN FOOL,' those were his words, said as a joke. You should have seen Phil's face. Her dad had to be talked down from putting a loafer in her husband's ass," he grunts.

"I'm going to say it. All of that could have been avoided if you had stopped being a damn fool and told Dani how you feel," I stress.

"Lord, man, Dani's married."

"Because you were a fucking fool. That woman is in love with you," I point out.

"You mean, GIRL," he corrects. "I'm not messing with our friend's daughter."

"Your self-sacrifice isn't noble when you and her are suffering."

"Okay, tell me this, why is Naomi questioning me about you?"

I should have called him out for flipping things to get out of the hot seat. Instead, I'm knocked off my train of thought.

"Yes, she's scoping you out. Now, why is that?" he inquires mockingly.

I regain my wits quickly.

"I'm guessing for the same reason why you sent her to me in the first place. But I'm willing to play the fool if it means a little while in heaven."

I pick up on Austin tapping on something while he considers my comment.

"She's coming to Vegas with Phil...to make sure the hotel is a good buy."

I smile at the longing in his tone. Things have been building between the two of them since Dani turned eighteen. Six years is a long time of denying oneself.

"Listen, we're old, we've had enough practice, why not, huh?" I ask with my own desire ringing true.

"Here's to playing the fool," Austin chuckles nervously. "God, I hate you, Zahn," he laughs before hanging up.

**

The entire ride, I try to plan what I'm going to say once I come face to face with Naomi. Let me tell you. I'm not ready. The butterflies in my stomach won't settle down. I low key search for Naomi in the house. I don't want to make it too obvious that I'm looking for her. With each room I enter, I come up empty. It's not long before I feel myself getting annoyed.

"She's not here."

I walk backwards to stand in the entryway of a room. Glancing in, Rivers is clearing a table. I don't pretend to act as if I'm innocent, not with her, at least.

"She's down at the site...been there every day since you've been gone."

"Why is she there?" I wonder.

"Well, she and her sister's helping to set up things. Good thing, too, because I was about to start shooting those lazy fuckers. Nobody could get their asses out of a hole long enough to work. Those two stepped in...and boom, action. Those two ain't nothing to mess with. They know how to give you the business in such a classy way, you wonder if they're actually telling you off. I like that shit," she praises with a nod.

Rivers just added another reason for me to head for the site. I can't explain my reaction once I arrive. The open area is completely transformed. Dazed, I slip off my four-wheeler. I don't respond to the people trying to get my attention. My brain can only do one thing at the moment.

"Naomi!!" I shout.

It takes me repeating five more times before I hear her over the activity.

"Here!!"

My cock instantly thickens at the sight of her dressed in a flowing, cream-colored mini dress. All I can think is my access to her pussy between her chocolate thighs has just gotten easier.

"Breath," I whisper as I walk towards her.

"First off, I'm so sorry."

Taken back, I damn near trip over my boots.

"Sorry?!" I repeat in a high pitch. I don't care about the eyes on me. I capture her face between my hands. My lips brush her mouth. Leaning back to put inches between us, I look into her eyes. "I don't think I've told you how beautifully amazing you are."

My smoothness takes her ability to speak. She moves her mouth, but nothing but a strange moan escape. I thumb her cheek.

"You have no idea how good it feels, knowing that you got me. Thank you."

"W, well, welcome," she smiles. "My sister helped, too," she adds as a second thought.

"Graham can thank her," I tease with a wink. Stepping back, "Show me around."

"Yeah," she nods.

I intertwin my hand with hers. I ignore Naomi's quick glimpse down. I'm not wasting any more time.

"So, the venders are on the right. Behind that are the showers. See there," she points as we stroll past. "I made sure they are set up in a way that people can see what's going on, no dark spots. Over there will be the stage. I heard there are to be poles?"

"For the dance," I explain.

"Poles? Ya'll having a stripping contest?" she jokes.

"No," I chuckle. "It's for a ritual. I can't tell you now," I mumble under my voice. I cut my eyes to hint off the reason why.

"Oh, gotach," she replies in a whisper. Getting loud, "Um, I was told no RVs are allowed, right...only tipis? So, they can pitch their tent anywhere in the open space, which is a lot. Port-a-potties are on the west and east of the site."

"Wonderful. I have stadium lighting coming, so the entire area will be lit up. There will be constant security, too," I add.

I change direction to head for the lodge. I'm glad to see that it's finally finished. Stooping down, I enter through the deer hid flap.

"Hold up," I demand, stopping Naomi from entering behind me.

"The lodge is a sacred place. Anyone can't just enter. You have to be part of the Tribe and invited by a medicine man or an elder."

She backs away as if she's been burned.

"Got it, um...I'll just..." she trails off to stroll away awkwardly.

It only takes me two steps to catch her. Grabbing her by the arm, I stop her to tower over her.

"You are so quick to accept defeat. It's like you're ready for the rejection."

"Old habits."

I enjoy her honestly. I'm not going to wonder what's changed. I'm just thankful that there is a change; one that I'm going to exploit to the fullest. I lick my lips.

"Listen," I begin with a quick glance around. "Be my guest. I mean, you're already my guest," I babble non slickly. I'm losing all my swag around the damn woman. "I'm inviting you to the festival and the Hunt."

"I'm not beating through the bush at night," she frowns.

I smirk, slowly.

"Why you see sex in everything?" she huffs.

"Because I'm all man," I answer while eating her up with my eyes. "I wanna beat the bush," I tease.

My heartbeat up ticks at her gaze, dropping to the bulge in my jeans before snapping her brown orbs away.

"We won't be in the woods, but in my tipi. The Hunt is for the boys to prove themselves alone. Travis and a few other fathers will come to camp, but that will be much later in the night. Until then, it will just be us, here...in case one of the boys need us," I motion at the sweat lodge, "We'll have a session in the lodge."

Naomi glances at the hut sceptically. "I don't smoke weed."

It takes me a second to catch on.

"I won't stop you for puffin on my pipe, but no, Naomi...nothing like that. I would never do anything to hurt you. Trust me," I stress as I touch her arm lightly. "I really think it will help you," I add.

She shifts her weight. "I need more than steam and St. Johns Wart."

"Then stop fighting me," I remark as I begin to walk backward.

For the next four hours, I remain only a few yards away from Naomi where ever she roams. Although I'm busy taking care of business and talking, I'm fully aware of her presence. I find myself watching her interact with others. The way she talks and carries herself, how she listens, the way she hides her eyes to keep others from seeing what's really going on in her mind, even how she laughs off the advances from the men, I see it all. I also notice the way she gravitates to the Fannie pack around her waist. I have no doubt her mood pills are housed safely within.

Piquing my interest, I continue to follow her around the site with my gaze. It's not long before I'm able to pick up on her body language. I marvel at the way she's ready to morph herself at the drop of a hat. It bothers and amazes me at the same time. I wonder if I've ever experienced Naomi, the *real* Naomi, or has she been treating me to her uncanny way of hiding behind a role?

It's only when she walks away does she allows her body to relax. A glimpse of her natural self appears on her relaxed face. A few times, I see her mouth moves as she mumbles under her breath. Then she's called upon, and like a switch, the curtain falls, and I see her change to fit the moment. It's only when she's with her sister that she's her most at ease. Even then, there's a lot more going on behind her smile than she's letting on. I want to know what.

NAOMI

"Zahn's sticking close."

"Huh?"

Sali sucks her teeth. "Don't play coy….and don't try to downplay it, either," she beams.

She dances over, locks our arms, and lays her head on my shoulder to stare at me with a goofy expression.

"Stop it," I hiss. "He'll know we're talking about him," I warn.

"So?" she laughs. "It's okay to like somebody," she teases. "You are human, sis."

"Never said I did."

"Then why you acting as if you don't care? Or that you don't want to feel all that thrusting, throbbing between your legs," she moans.

"I can't stand your ass," I grunt.

Unfazed, she twirls away only to come back to simulate fucking by thrusting her hips for all to see. Quickly, my eyes dart over to where I know Zahn is talking. Sure enough, he's watching and smiling at her antics.

"Stop," I demand as I take a swat at her. "I'm not running after you. Quit it."

"He's gonna fuck you up when he gets it. He looks like the kinda guy that's going to turn you out," she warns with a wink.

Blocking her from his line of vision, "If he fucks how he kisses, I know for a fact-"

Suddenly, her hand pops up into my face. "Hold it! You kissed him? I'm sharing all my tea with you, and you didn't tell me?"

"For the record, I never called you for tea time. That was all you," I point out.

For a second, Sali is silent. I hate the way she looks at Zahn than back to me. She's making damn sure he knows he's the topic of our conversation.

"He left and came back knowing what he wants...and that's YOU."

No longer acting, I step nearer to Sali. "You think so? I mean, *really*, Sali?"

Her smile falls from her lips. She blinks as if she's noticing me for the first time.

"You actually like him, don't you?" she presses, although she doesn't let me answer. "Listen, I've picked up a lot about Zahn from Graham and the others. From what I hear, he's good people, like a damn saint, ...and he plays to win. If it's sex, make sure he UNDERSTANDS it's just that...and make sure it STAYS that way," she says, slowly.

"Dick isn't going to turn my head," I scoff. "I have a role waiting for me."

"Then have fun, then."

See, I hear her response, but you don't know my sister. I can tell by the way Sali said that, she thinks I'm full of shit.

**

Alight, maybe there's just a hint of shit. My nervousness is mounting. My lack of focus is growing as time ticks closer. After Zahn's invite yesterday, my imagination has been running wild of what to expect. It's the elephant in the room that we've both have danced around all day during my lessons.

I experienced a moment of worry that things were going to fall through. I didn't even realize I had been holding my breath as I watched Zahn walk away to take a call. To peg him as a passive man is a colossal mistake. It was then that I saw him for the man he can be. Whoever he was cursing out in a deep, even tone under his breath in hopes that I won't hear had a fear of God put in them.

"YOU'RE DUMB AS A JACKRABBIT. LISTEN, CHICKEN SHIT. I TOLD YOU WHAT I WANTED. ANYTHING SHORT, AND I'M GOING TO SKIN YOUR ASS. OH, YOU PUTTING A LITTLE BASS IN YOUR VOICE, HUH? DON'T BACK PADDLE NOW. I'LL BE BY LATER TO HELP CLEAR THAT UP FOR YOU."

A shiver ran down my spine. I pride myself on being able to slip in and out of character. The way Zahn could hide his anger, going from growling and threatening back to the smiling, smooth-talking, teasing man was downright creepy. Long after he left to fuck up whomever, I lifted wondering if I was smart to engage in anything more than the lessons I'm here for.

"It's not like I'm giving up my life for sex...no matter how good it may be," I remind myself with a shrug.

To be honest, nothing short of witnessing him murder somebody would have turned my head. All the teasing, touching, those kisses combined with my own lack of sex, created an excitement that's driving me crazy. That excitement grew tenfold at the sound of his deep laughter echoing from downstairs. I cracked my room door to listen to him, and Rivers tit for tat. Shortly after, Zahn broke away from the verbal back and forth to get ready for later. That was the cue for the butterflies in my stomach to flutter. I could barely concentrate on my lines or taking calls for the next two hours. I welcomed the knock at my door.

"Yeah."

Sticking her head in the door, "Rivers want us," Sali announces.

"Are we in trouble?"

Sali shrugs. Rivers meets us at the foot of the stairs to lead us into a small side room that I've passed by many times but never noticed it. Sali and I enter and wait for the older woman to take a seat behind a sewing table. With no other place to sit, my sister and I stand.

"I'm not one to beat around the bush, so I'll get to it. The boys won't tell you, but I'm not pussy focused, so I will. The two of you came here for one thing, but it seems you'll be riding a lot more than horses," she smirks.

Now, if it were anyone else than this crusty old woman, I would be in my feelings. Rivers has become the mature Mama that I needed in my life. The one that would have given it to me straight, the one that would have always had my back and front…and wouldn't have used me for all I was worth like my parents had.

She gestures with a hand to two wrapped lumps on the table.

"The boys asked me to make these for you for the festival. You might see deerskin and pretty bead working…but it's more than that. What they are doing in inviting the two of you is MORE than that. What goes on there... at the site isn't like a pow-wow opened to any wanna be Native. There are no tickets being sold at a gate to let any and all in. It is sacred...and if they are inviting you, dressing you, welcoming you into their tipis, it is a statement that all will take note of."

Rivers stands, slowly — her tiny eyes darts between Sali and me to burn into our coronas.

"You will listen to your man. If he tells you to stay, sit, and shut up, you better do it. You will not embarrass them before the Tribe, because everyone will be watching. Do not question them in front of others. You let that question burn a hole in your tongue if need be. If something happens, you stick to us," she instructions.

I exchange a glance with Sali.

"Like what?"

Sali gets the questions out before me.

Something strange flickers across Rivers' wrinkled face. I can tell she's considering her answer.

"This festival will bring many things on the wind. Now, wear these with pride. I know my boys will be proud," she smiles as she pushes the piles across the table towards us.

Neither I or Sali reach for the packages. I know we're both weighing the cost of going through with everything. Our idea of fun, food, and sex isn't the same after all that's been said. I'm also thinking about Zahn's phone conversation from earlier and his family drama. Is that what Rivers is hinting at?

Sali reaches for her package, while I hesitate.

"Should I worry?" I wonder.

Rivers leans in a bit. "Zahn is a bastard, and a patient one, too. There's a ruthless motherfucker behind his smile and muscle. Everyone around here knows it...and the old misses is crazy to believe she's going to rule the hen house again...but YOU, YOU don't have nothing to fear, baby girl," she nods as she pushes my package to my hand.

I grip the package. However, I linger in the room long after Rivers and Sali leave.

CHAPTER NINE

ZAHN

She's late. Then again, Naomi is a woman of color, so maybe I shouldn't be too worried. I made sure to mark the path through the woods to ensure she didn't get lost. I would have brought her here myself if not for wanting time alone to settle myself. Too much shit at one time, when all I want to do is spend my days joking around with Naomi. It was a shock to the system when I admitted to myself that I long for more than the work of the farm and the Tribe. I actually want something that's my own...for me.

I could have stayed longer in the lake I bathed in, but the desire to get tonight right had me moving my ass. Dipping back into the tipi, I glance around. It's not as if anything has moved. I'm just too nervous to stay still. The baying noise from my stallion alerts me that someone is coming. Not too quickly, I come back out only in time to see Naomi break through the tree line. I whistle a command that causes her mare to freeze. Getting on my horse, I ride over to get her. Under the blinding stadium light, I'm able to take in the sight of Naomi long before I reach her.

I chuckle at her, tugging at the hem of her dress. The action draws my eyes to her toned, chocolate thigh.

"I think it's missing a few yards."

Angling my head, I get a clear view of her white cotton underwear.

"No, it's just right," I laugh.

She shifts, but there's nothing she can do. I dance my horse to her side. I can't get enough of her. The soft deerskin material hugs her body and stretches over her breast and hips. The beadwork of Rivers around the neckline is similar to my necklace, but she still managed to make Naomi's dress unique.

"You look even better than I imagined," I say while taking the reins of her horse.

Absentmindedly, she touches the end of one of the braids. I smile, knowing she must really like me to let me see her natural neck length hair.

Slow, I put our horses into motion for my tipi.

"I thought we would be out here alone."

I follow her gaze to the three tipis standing far away from mine.

"We are. The Hunt started at sundown. The guys came out to put those up. Since he has Sali, one belongs to Graham. Gil and Wes are sharing. The other is for their dad, Travis, their Mom, and Rivers."

"Have I seen their Mom?"

"She's been seeing about Travis' sister. They don't talk too much about the woman, but his sister seems to be worse off. I'll make sure you meet his wife when she comes," I promise.

"Damn, it's big," she breathes.

I chuckle. Catching her side-eye, "You should know better by now," I laugh.

"The TIPI is bigger than I expected," she laughs.

Already, I'm beginning to relax while the sexual tension between us grows. I take joy in sharing my world, my culture with her.

"They had to be. Back in the day, an entire TIYOSPAYE, or family would share one. The tipis are clustered into family OSPAYE or groups. The painting on the deerskin is like an address to let all know who lives there."

After we both slide from the horses, she takes her time examining the hand painting on my tipi. The images of war, hunting, and worship of the moon cover the outside of the tipi. By the time she reaches the front flap, I'm ready to welcome her.

"Ready?"

She nods. Like earlier, I entwin my hands in hers to walk over to the sweat lodge. I pause at the opening. Bending down, I pick up the bundle of sage I had burning before she got here. I know she's clueless of the words I'm speaking in my Native language, but Naomi listens intently anyway. She breathes in deeply of the smoke as I start from her head to her moccasin covered feet.

Switching back to English, "Naomi, I cover you. No longer do you move through this world alone. I accept you. Do you accept me?"

I'm sure she doesn't realize the magnitude of what's happening.

"Yes," she speaks firmly.

"Listen, no judgment. Whatever is spoken in the lodge during meditation STAYS here...so be yourself, don't hold back...come out better, whole. I hope I can trust you," I add.

I like the fact she takes a second to consider both my words and her response.

"Have you done this before...with another woman?"

My answer is going to reveal a lot.

"You're my first."

I want to add, "AND MY LAST," but I don't. I watch an emotion play out across Naomi's face before she answers.

"You can trust me," she promises.

Wrapping my arm around her waist, I lead her through the flap. I give her time to look around the open space while I add more water to the cluster of hot rocks in the middle of the room.

"Wow, it's hot as h- Can I curse?" She wonders.

"Why the hell not?" I reply. "Take a seat," I order. "Drink this."

Naomi takes the mug, sniffs, and hesitates.

"It's just an herbal tea…NON-CANNABIS, no mushrooms, either. I'll never do anything to hurt you.

"Hum, tastes good," she smiles as she brings the rim back up for another gulp.

I take up my cup as I sit across from her. I cut the chatter while we finish the tea. The drink will help to relax us. I made sure to alter the mixture of plants to dilute the power of the tea. I want to loosen our tongues and remove the fear, not go on a mental trip.

We both stare into the glowing red pile of rocks, and the rising steam. It's not long before beads of sweat cover my brow. Reaching over my head, I remove my shirt to toss to the ground — a loud intake of breath echoes through the place. I find her wide eyes glued to my chest. I don't know if she's shocked by the tattoos covering my shoulder and forearms? Or is it the scars I wear with pride on my chest.

"You can ask me whatever," I remind her.

"What's the story?"

I touch the ugly scars on the left of my chest with my fingers.

"It's the Lakota's most sacred ritual called the Sun Dance. Bungy like cords are attached to a tall pole. The other end is attached to the chest with bird talons. Young boys, warriors dance around the pole…going in, towards the pole, then they pull back, hanging there, pulling the flesh," I explain.

"Those poles outside are for that?"

"Yes. Although I cover you, you still can't attend," I warn.

"I don't want to," with a start, she continues, "not that I'm downing it," she adds in a rush. "Africans have their way of doing things, hell all cultures do," she finishes in a mumble, still staring, "Nice ink."

I flex my arms, and she pretends to faint. I like the joking and easy-going vibe so far. This is what I wanted to see…experience with Naomi to figure out if my attraction stopped at the flesh or if there is more drawing me to her. I wait for her to get the courage to ask me her next questions. I can wait to ask her mine.

"Why are you stretching yourself so thin?"

I shrug, dropping my gaze. I wish to God she would have started with a topic less heavy.

"That doesn't count as an answer," she smirks.

"I'll remind you of that later," I huff. A loud sign escapes my lips. "Although the Lakota is my Tribe, because of my family, I'm not fully accepted. I know that. I understand why, but a person still wants to be a part. I do it out of pride…and out of that deep desire," I admit.

I search her face to see if she understands me. I'm taken back by the sadness my honest creates.

"You'll never please them, so don't try too hard. Be happy with the few that love you for you, instead of killing yourself to get it all."

I open my mouth, then close it. Things could go sideways, depending on how Naomi reacts.

"Is it just you and your sister?" I inquire as I ease into it.

"Yeah."

"I'm sorry. When did your parents die?" I question as if I didn't know they are alive and kicking.

"They haven't, but I don't have any contact with them."

"Why? What caused the falling out?"

I wonder if Naomi even heard my question when she goes silent. She stares into the glowing rocks. I can hear the change in her breathing. I'm knocking on a door that she keeps lock, and I can tell the idea of cracking it open to peer inside is painful.

"Do you know your birth mother?"

Her question shocks me for a second.

"No," I frown.

I wish she would look up so I can read what's going on with her through her eyes.

"Why not?"

I ponder for a moment. "I wanted to once I came to grips with the fact that Abby would never be a mother to me. I've lived all my life right here in the area. I didn't even go to college. If my mother ever wanted to find me, I'm in plain sight...but she didn't, so why seek a person that doesn't want to know me?"

"Smart," she mumbles with a nod. "You saved yourself a lot of pain, Zahn. You're blessed with smarts that I wasn't. I loved, cherished, and trusted my parents. If they said work, I worked, and I would be sooo tired. If they said smile, I did it till my jaws hurt. If they said to trust someone...to be quiet when you try to tell them what's being done to you, I trusted, I was quiet... and they profited," she pauses to steal a glimpse of my stone face. "Having a family is overrated when the predators are living in the house with you. Now, they're living overseas on the money I've worked for, and they stole from me."

"Is that why you left Hollywood?" I question.

Naomi laughs. A twisted, hurtful sound. "Have I told you I love the way you talk? You make things sound so...nice. LEFT HOLLYWOOD," she repeats. "So sweet and pure. You mean, is that why I got strung out, lost the little, I did have, and hit rock bottom? Why, yes, Zahn. Being raped by powerful movie executives and producers while making my parents rich could have had something to do with it."

"I'm so s-"

She gives me a palm. "No," she snaps. "It's not your fault. Please don't...I'm just," she says on a loud exhale and a shake of her head.

I clamp my mouth down to keep from saying, I UNDERSTAND when I don't. Naomi's pain is unique to her. I won't dismiss it in such a dumb way.

"Before you got mad when I said something about you being a Mom. Your Mom... your parents' sins aren't yours, Naomi. That's all them."

Her eyes dart to glare at me. I freeze under her hard stare. I've managed to fuck up after all. Suddenly, her brown eyes become cloudy and wet. The tea is allowing her to acknowledge and speak truths that were hidden.

"I don't like it here," she announces, pulling at the neckline of her dress. "Fucking drink," she screams, jumping to her feet.

I move to block her from running. She dodges to the left to crash into my unmovable body. Frustrated, she punches me. Later, I'll recall her hard right to my jaw. Her hands claw at a pouch she pinned to her dress. My large hand closes over her shaking one.

"I wouldn't mix the pills and the tea," I add enough uncertainty to my voice to make the lie believable.

"Jesus," she howls in pain.

Snatching her hand from mine, Naomi power walks to the back of the lodge. Frantically, she pulls at her hair. When she begins to beat the side of her head, I rush to her. I seize her hand in mid-air to fasten it to her side. It takes nothing to subdue her. I follow her to the rug covered ground while she curses and yells to the heavens.

Finally having enough, I shake the shit out of her. Her head wobbles on her shoulders till she quiets down a bit.

"Say it!" I scream into her face.

Determined, her full lips form a firm line. Tears stream down her face. Half of me wants to back off, let her continue to live with the paralyzing hurt of the memory. Yet, the crushing anguish written in the lines etched on her face can't be ignored.

Once again, I begin to shake and order her to speak.

"SPEAK, DAMN IT!! LET IT OUT, NAOMI. LET IT GO!!"

There is no denying the power of the herbs. It's a powerful truth serum that's been used for years. Whatever the soul is hiding, whatever is in the heart, will come to light.

Naomi's truth comes out like an eruption that rocks us both. My eyes widen. Time and my heart stop. I must have heard her wrong.

"I killed her," she repeats on a trembling, tear-filled whisper. "I...I, I killed her," she admits, again.

The admission is the key to the floodgates. All I can do is hold on to her. I lose track of time in the hot silence. I don't have to urge her to talk. Like removing a band-aid, Naomi doesn't want to stop now that she's started. I push up her slumped over body upright to face me.

"Who did you kill?"

Her eyes roam around the lodge as if she had forgotten where she was.

"I...I had been so excited, sooo excited," she stresses. "Wh, when I found out. I felt that this was what I needed to force me to get right," she moans.

Suddenly, her gaze fastens on an unseen object, an invisible place, time that has haunted her.

"I had stopped using once I found out. I was still on the streets. I didn't care. I would figure that part out. All I wanted was the baby. I, I even stole a little onesie. It had, MOM'S WORLD, printed on it," she smiles through the tears, only to pause, her brow creasing in pain. "But then it happened. A, a, at first, I didn't know what was going on. There was a sharp stab in my stomach, then a gush and....," she inhales, "there she was," she says as she looks down into her open, empty hands.

Afraid to break the flow, I remain still. I, too, have traveled back in time to watch the memory unfold.

"She was so, so, SO small," Naomi cries. "I mean, in one hand, she could fit...b, but she...was not all right. Her hands were...and her head was..." she trails off, not going into detail. "And the sound, the sound she made, I'll never, EVER forget it. She was trying, but she wasn't going to be able to liv, not like, like that," she whispers.

I can hear her swallow. I already know how the story ends.

"So, ...I, I just, I just, um, I," stammers Naomi.

I watch while she covers her left hand with her right to mimic her suffocating the child. Crying, she brings her clasped hands to her chest as she rocks her lost baby girl. Never had I thought that she was carrying such a weight. I, like the rest of the world, only knew the beautiful actress that fell on rough times.

"You're still young, Naomi," I point out in hopes to console her.

"No," she speaks in a hoarse tone. "A shot cleared up the gonorrhea. I wasn't so lucky with the case of Pelvic Inflammatory Disease. The meds cleared it up, but I had it so long that the scarring on my tubes... I WON'T be given another chance."

I scrub my hand down my face. How much more can this woman be fucked over? My heart is bleeding for her. To have her one ray of hope, to have her chance at love, and to be loved stripped away from her when she needed it most is beyond words.

Silently, I rise. Later, I return with a cold bottle of water. Naomi doesn't even look at me when I pass it to her. I wait till she takes a few sips before I squash the distance building between us.

"Hey," I begin while forcing her to acknowledge me with a finger under her chin. "This can't do. I can't do you going back into your mental cage and cutting me out." I grip her shoulders, pinning her with my gaze. I confess a dark secret. "I have no room to judge you. I've killed, and if need be, I'm making plans to kill again. Over LAND, Naomi. Over MONEY. You know my secret, and I know yours. I don't see you any different from the woman of my dreams. I just want to love you more, protect you more, be there for you more," I admit, wiping a tear from her cheek.

I'm not surprised she's unable to speak. She's searching my face for a lie. She won't find one.

NAOMI

I must have lost my mind. How could I have told Zahn my darkest secret? What I've spent thousands of dollars and wasted hours laying on a couch dancing around, I've just spilled to him. Not even Sali knows the horror I just spoke of.

MY CHEST IS GOING TO EXPLODE. I'M GOING TO DIE, WHICH WOULD BE A FITTING END FOR ME. I DID THAT. I KILLED MY...JESUS, HELP ME, PLEASE. I KNOW I DON'T DESERVE IT, BUT PLEASE...HAVE MERCY. WHY IS HE SAYING THIS? WHY IS ZAHN TELLING ME, IT'S ALL OKAY? HIS TOUCH IS TORTURE. HIS WORDS ARE LIKE KNIVES. THIS, TOO, MUST BE MY PUNISHMENT, RIGHT GOD?

While I see myself dying of a heart attack, the other voice is trying to convince me that I'm not. That what I'm experiencing is one hell of a panic attack.

"SHUT UP!" I shout as I cover my ears.

I know the voices battling in my mind won't obey, but I'm thankful that Zahn does. I'm scared to close my eyes, because her tiny form will be there, waiting. I'm hot. The dress that felt so soft has now become so constricting. Without thought, I tug free of it. Casting it aside, I get to my feet in nothing but my bra and panties. I eye the flap that leads to outside, but I know Zahn won't let me go. I can feel his gaze on my sweaty skin, watching me. I have to force myself to focus when I notice his lips moving.

"Naomi."

His hands are up, open with the palms facing me in a sign of surrender.

"It wasn't your faul-"

Knowing the lie he's about to speak, I leap at him. My arms kick into a windmill motion to deliver as many punches before I back away spent. I can barely make out his face through my tears. After all of that, Zahn is still here, standing in the midst of my raging hurricane.

"How the fuck wasn't, isn't my fault. I was the one shooting up. I was the one fucking on the streets for my next hit."

I notice the slight uptick of his eyebrow.

"Oh, yes," I chuckle, harshly. "Oh, you thought I was being passed around by rich men when I was off the radar? Oh no, I was taking some of the nastiest dick in alleys, crack houses, tables in the park," I list. "This," I motion with a sweep of my hand, "is a fantasy. I'm nothing, NOTHING but a bitch in sheep's clothing. So, don't tell me what happened to her wasn't my fault. I said I was going to be better than my own mother. I promised that I was going to protect her, love her...and I, I, couldn't," I cry, spit flying in every direction.

For moment, it's just the sound of my whining filling the space until Zahn speaks.

"You're right. You want the truth?"

His question jars me. I taste the salty tears lingering on my lip. Changing my stance, I look him in the face.

"Yes," I nod.

He doesn't hesitate.

"You were a dumb bitch."

I'm taken back by the anger in his words. His handsome face wrinkles and twists with rage as it comes to the surface.

"How the hell are you going to be a whore and not protect from getting knocked up? Whatcha thought was going to happen, huh? That poor girl was dead no matter what. If you did go full term, she would have been fucked in some way, because you think you were going to be able to stop, just like that?"

"I had stopped. I was cleaning myself up," I say firmly.

"Yeah, you did...but it was too late. The damage was done." Switching gears, "Why didn't you get off the streets? Why didn't you take your ass to live with your sister?" He presses.

"I wanted to do it on my own," I answer.

Zahn tilts his head while narrowing his gaze. "The truth," he snaps, making me jump.

"Shame," I blurt out. "I didn't want Sali to see me…like…that," I pause to inhale. "I, maybe if I had, when I found out instead of staying out there for months, I could have-"

"She might have lived. So, that's another stone, another knot in the noose around your neck. You've been allowing the ghost of your past to kill you slowly," he begins.

I watch while he strolls off. Bending, he goes to the pile of rocks not being used to create steam to pick out a few. Carefully, he positions his shirt open on the ground to place each one in. Then he knots it close, securing the rocks inside.

"Do you want to die?"

I blink.

"To atone, to pay for what you've done, do you want to give up the life God has given back to you?"

He stands to come back to tower over me with the heavy bundle in his hand.

"I heard it said that He doesn't make mistakes, even if we don't understand the reasons why. I'm not Godly. I'm just trying to speak in a way for you to understand me. Naomi, all that time you were on the streets, doing what you were doing, you could have died. You could have picked up something that would have killed you later, but you didn't. Why? Why do you still have a life? Why have you been given another chance to live, to work? But you have to be willing to ingest, accept, own what you've done, the mistakes you've made…or you can go on and die for it all."

I open my mouth to ask a question, but he cuts me off. "Don't answer now."

Zahn grips my hand. I'm in a daze as he leads me out of the sweat lodge. I train my eyes on the inky sky above while he calls for his horse. Quickly, he places me into the saddle. Not getting behind me, he takes up the reigns and begins to lead the horse on foot. The temperature has dropped. Or maybe it's the fact that I'm no longer hot from the steam of the lodge.

No matter. I welcome the change. It helps to calm me down a bit. Lost in my thoughts, I don't even watch where Zahn is taking me. It isn't until we stop do I look around to find we've crossed the open field, went through the woods, and are now at a water source. It could be a stream or lake. It's too dark to tell.

"Come on?" he orders.

I take his hand to slip from the saddle. As if I weigh nothing, Zahn picks me up to carry me up a grassy hill. Once there, he places me back on my feet.

He passes me the sack of rocks. "Hold on to your shame, hurt, guilt, the anger of your parents, and sink to the bottom. Let it all kill you. Or you let it all go to remain at the bottom and come back to life. Your choice."

I JUST KNOW HE ISN'T GOING TO...WHY IS HE TYING A ROPE AROUND MY-

My scream of terror blots out the voices in my mind when he pushes me off the hill to fall into the waters below. The impact stings. The coldness chills me to the bone as I'm weighed down to the bottom.

HOW DEEP IS THIS WATER? I wonder.

Why the hell is that what I'm thinking about? Shouldn't I be fighting to get loose? Yet, I'm not. I let the darkness, the quiet engulfs me. There's a peace... a calmness that calls to me. With ease, I can give in to its song. I crack my eyes to survey what could become my final resting place.

I'll swear by it whenever I retell the story. I know it's not an overactive mind or an illusion. I'm convinced, without a doubt that the light, the touch, and the presence so clear is there with me in the cold, watery depths. She's so pretty. Her touch so solid as she pulls me to her little body. There's no resistance on my part. Wide-eyed, I listen to her whisper in my ear. There's a tugging on the rope around my waist. Even though she's freed me, I still hold onto the rope.

Suddenly, she backs away. Her smile is so bright, so innocent...so happy. In a trance, I watch my little girl float away, to leave me once again.

"Bye, mama," a voice echoes.

My lungs are burning like a motherfucker, but I linger there until her form is wholly swallowed up by the darkness. The fear hits me all at once. Do I want to die, follow my baby into the dark unknown?

I LOVE YOU. BYE, BABY.

I let go of the rope. I let go of it all. Frantic for air, I explode through the surface.

"NAOMI! NAOMI!!!"

Zahn screaming my name from somewhere nearby is the first thing that I hear. I got to tell you. It feels so good. To be hearing, seeing, feeling, and to be able to recognize that he's going crazy with dread that I might have chosen death because he cares. It's a damn good feeling.

"Over here," I manage to croak out in the direction he's floating.

"Thank you," he says as he treads the water towards me.

I don't know who he's thanking, but I'm doing a lot of that myself. Call me crazy, but I feel reborn. Even the night sky above appears to be new. All I want to do is stare at it. Flopping over onto my back, I do just that as I float, lifeless upon the water.

CHAPTER TEN

ZAHN

I didn't ask, and Naomi didn't tell me what happened. Once I made it to her side, I found her floating, gazing up at the sky. Neither one of us spoke long after returning to my tipi. I must have been out of my goddamn mind pushing her like that. I'm just thankful I didn't have to explain her dead body.

"I'll be back," I announce.

Wes and Gil know not to enter a tipi without being welcomed; however, I'm not taking the chance they'll break from protocol. All I know is I'm thankful for a reason to leave. We both need space, after all, that's occurred. I feel my age, and from the looks of Naomi's puffy eyes and worn expression, she needs the quiet, too.

"We saw you two come back. Everything okay?"

I nod my answer to Wes' question. He won't push for details.

"Well, none of the boys have sent up a flare, so alls good," Wes continues.

I nod again while I glance around the open area.

"Where's your dad?"

The exchange between the brothers doesn't go unnoticed.

"He's dealing with something about his sister," replies Gil.

"Your mom is visiting her. I know the old lady is sick, is she doing worse?"

"Nah, she's a tough one. Nothing like that," Gil waves me off. "We'll let you get back to-"

"She wants to come, our aunt...to the festival," interjects Wes. He's not ready to switch topics, which seems to piss off Gil. "It's Rivers idea."

I take a second to examine the brothers. "Let her come if she wants to. If she needs extra help because of her condition, we all can see to her," I shrug.

"We'll take care of her, plus there's Rivers," Wes points out.

"But she probably won't come, so forget it," adds Gil, firmly. This time, he does change the topic. "Sali sent this for Naomi."

I take the small backpack from his hand. Neither one is making sense, and frankly, I don't have the energy to try to figure out what the hell they're up to. I know I'm tired when I let them leave without asking for an update on the tasks they've been working on in my favor. All I want is the welcomed silence of the night. All I want is to be left alone to process my thoughts and the events for tonight.

It's only the fact that Naomi might be hungry that forces me back into the tipi.

"Is something wrong?" I inquire upon finding her standing in the middle of the area.

"Just taking everything in. This is a nice setup," she praises.

I carpeted the grassy ground with rugs. Space for a fire in the middle was all that was left uncovered. Plush pillows are tossed throughout. I even brought in a large ice chest for drinks.

"I was imaging sleeping bags on the ground," she admits.

"A stiff dick is all I want to wake up with, so I'll pass on that," I joke.

Unlike before, Naomi laughs. There's an evident change in her.

"Your sister sent this," I say as I offer her the bag.

"I left it on the table," she smiles.

After she takes it, she begins to rub her left wrists absentmindedly. It's an action she's been doing off and on since returning from the water.

"Did you hurt yourself?"

I question, causing her to realize what she was doing. Her beaming smile is something to behold, I tell you.

"No," she chuckles while looking at her wrist. "I'm not hurt. It's from something that happened underwater."

DON'T ASK, a voice reminds me.

I'm not given a chance to argue. All debating ceases when Naomi glides over, rolls up on the tips of her toes, and kisses me lightly on the lips.

"Thank you," she breaths before putting unwelcome space between us. "So, who threw you in the water?"

I chuckle. "Seemed too scripted, huh?"

"Chapter and verse."

I stroll over to the insulated pouch keeping our burgers and fries warm.

"It was Bradley, my dad...and yeah, Travis was there, too. I was about 7, maybe 8. I was only happy when Bradley was home. When he was gone, working, I got no relief at home or school. That's a lot for a kid, and after years of it, I became irate, mean, violent at times. They both brought me out here, gave me a good talking to when spanking me didn't work anymore. They gave me a choice."

"And you chose, to live, obviously," she remarks while taking the food.

"Yeah," I reply as I take a seat next to her. "They say those waters is like a looking glass. In it, you'll face the ghosts within your soul. Either you'll win the battle, or you'll lose all to it. I was never the same after that day," I finish with a forlong gaze.

"Teaching me how to ride, and now this...you've helped me in ways you can't even imagine, Zahn."

JESUS, I'M STARING AT HER LIPS. SHE'S JUST GONE THROUGH AN EMOTIONAL EXPERIENCE, AND I'M HERE FANTASIZING ABOUT FUCKING HER.

"No sexual comeback?"

I drop my eyes to keep my desire hidden.

"Not tonight, but I'll be back in form tomorrow," I promise.

It's the stillness that causes me to look up. She doesn't have to say a word.

"Naomi," I start slowly, so she hears me. "I'm not treating you differently because you haven't changed. You're still beautiful, sexy, smart. You're broken, bruised, emotional, and I won't use that to my advantage. I don't want you laying down with me to be another mistake you add to your list," I explain.

Her brown eyes dart across my face.

"You say all the right things, Zahn...you really do...and I want to believe, sooo bad-"

"But?"

She shakes her head while glancing away on a sigh.

"Can you make it last?" She finally asks.

I'm gut-punched. I have to fight hard to control my breathing. Naomi's one questions hold all my dreams, wants, and needs.

"For as long as you want it."

I mean this shit. If she wants me, I'm all in. Never has there been a woman I'm willing to put everything in the backseat for. For once, I can see myself living a life for me and not for others.

NAOMI

I'm a ball of nerves. That's the only way to describe the feelings raging within me. Although Zahn said he was still into me, I can't stop wondering if it's a lie. I watch his every move for the next two days. I find myself picking apart every facial reaction and comment, trying to figure out if things have changed. The fear that he's going to expose my past to others or the media kept me up at night. I followed him each time he left the tipi to work with the others on getting the festival ready. I'm sure I was annoying the hell out him by being up his ass. However, he would smile without a nasty word. His hands were constantly on me in hopes of proving to me there was nothing to worry about.

The constant attention and time spent did more than calm me. It also made me want Zahn to the point that I'm going out of my mind wondering, fantasizing if and when we had sex, how would it be? Even though we've had opportunity, to finally get it on, he's given me nothing more than a kiss. At first, I found his patients sweet. Most men would jump a woman's bones at the first opportunity. The fact that they are fucking an emotional wreck of a woman is the last thing on a man's mind as long as he gets a nut.

Rolling over, I listen to the same birds that seem to greet us every morning. This time, there are voices of others working to set up their tipis and vendor sites today. The boys are set to return from the hunt by late noon. If all went well, each boy would have deer meat with them that will be cooked over fire pits to feed the Tribe on the first night of the festival. Soon, Zahn will get up, get dressed to leave to assist and oversee the work.

It was by no mistake that I fell asleep on his pallet. The days had turned colder. Even though Zahn made sure to keep the wood on the fire, I still used the drop in temperature as an accuse to nuzzle. Tucked under his arm, we watched the 90's *Martin* sitcom. I relaxed in his warmth and enjoyed the deep rumble of his laughter in his chest. Still, he did nothing to progress things between us to my frustration. Trust me, I understand the reason for his noble actions. I just want it to stop.

A shiver tickles my spine. Scooting closer, I plaster my body to his strong back. I snake my arm around him to drape over his waist. While I'm dressed in a light cotton night gown, Zahn is sleeping in just a pair of low riding pajama pants. I chew on the bottom of my lip as I consider my next move. I better not wait too long, though. People around here act as if they can't do shit on their own.

It's as if my fingers have a mind of their own when they begin to brush over his taunt stomach. Firm, lean, Zahn is in amazing shape to be 48 years old. I pride myself for going slow when all I want to do is finally being an end to my 3-year drought. North or South? I close my eyes, take a deep breath, say a silent prayer that I don't make a fool out of myself, and choose south. I bury my face against his hard back as my hand travels lower, over the waistline of his pants to reach his...

Suddenly, Zahn's large hand covers mine to stop my progress. I instantly feel the sting of rejection and shame. I try to snatch my hand free, but he refuses to let go. He moves my hand upward, then down again....and into his pants. The heat of his body is tense. In control, he cuffs my hand around his stiff dick before he sets me free.

"Whatever you want, Naomi," he whispers.

"I want everything, all of you...I want to *feel* you, see you," I breathe against his skin.

Still on his side, Zahn removes his pants before rolling over to face me. He doesn't have to give me an open invite. Nor do I waste anytime playing the shy girl. My hot eyes roam over his body to get a visual of what I'm still holding tightly in my hand.

"Is it good enough?" he questions.

My eyes widen a fraction as he makes his dick jerk in my grip.

"It's been 3 years, Zahn. Yes, you're more than good enough, might me too good," I add in a low voice.

"Hum, so this isn't a casual fuck."

I won't comment. I won't confirm that he's right.

"Thank you," he whispers as he draws me closer, "for honoring me in such a way."

Lord, why can't he be a dick about this? Why must he be so damn caring, so fuckin' perfect.

"What do you like? Teach me how to love your body."

At my stunned silence, he continues. "Can I nibble?"

"Yes."

"Are your nipples sensitive and like to me sucked?" he asks as he brushes my chest, lightly.

"Yes," I moan.

"What about here?"

He touches the apex at my thighs.

"Can I finger you?"

I let my legs parting be his answer to his question. Never have I seen such lust, desire etched on a man's face till Zahn. Nor have I've felt such heat like what I'm feeling from just his eyes staring at my shaved pussy. He seems to be in awe, as if he's seeing one for the first time.

His fingertip brushes my clit, causing me to jerk.

"Don't make it too easy for me. I want to work to make you cum. I'll have to take my time tasting this to get you open for me."

"How do you know when I've cum?"

I know I didn't just say...fuck, yes I did.

The expression on his face tells me all I need to know. Suddenly, Zahn smiles.

"No," he demands as he seizes my hands from covering my face in embarrassment. "No, Naomi. Thank you for being honest...and thank you for letting me be your first. I promise, you'll never forget this day...or me."

From the moment Zahn's lips cover mine, I swear to God that this man can not be human. The things just his kiss is making me feel is more than anything a man should be able to do. His touch is so light between my legs. Wanting more, I open them wider, begging for him to explore.

"Yes," I hiss as one of his finger slides over my wetness to enter me. "Fuck, me," I moan as I bury my face in the creak of his neck.

Quickly, I want more. I want to be stretched, filled and his finger isn't doing enough.

"More," I moan while pumping my hips to his rhythm.

Giving me what I need, another finger enters me as Zahn fucks me hard. He moves his body a bit lower to capture my hardened nipple. I love the combination of the sensations from his hard ass suckle and the fucking of my pussy with his fingers.

"O, what is that?"

I try to lean up to get a look at what he's doing between my legs that has my body tingling and my head swimming. I need to know so I can repeat the action whenever I'm alone. I catch just enough to see Zahn's thumb moving against my clit before I fall back.

"Open wider."

I'm about to dislocate my legs, I toss them open so wide.

"Ah, there it is. I've found it," he chuckles.

"What? Oh, God I, I"

"From the look of you, you'll know in a few seconds," he promises as he shifts his hand to pump my pussy harder.

Dropping his head, he rolls my nipple in between his teeth, then bites.

"HEAVEN HELP Mmmmm."

Is the world shaking? No, no, I'm shaking. Scared I try to dislodge his hand, but he refuses to give in.

"It's alright. Let it wash over you," he whispers as he holds onto me.

Wide eyed and flabbergasted, I stare into Zahn's face. I'm thankful that he's not his wise ass self, because I know I must look crazy right about now. To be as old as I am, and to have never experienced a true orgasm until now. Or the fact that I didn't even know my body could feel this way is sad.

"You like that?"

"Damn near killed me," I answer in a rush.

"Oh, that's coming later," he promises.

"Hold up," I shout at the sight of him moving his head downward.

"Just lay back and relax," he orders. He forces me to obey with a firm shove to the chest.

I'm scared. I'm scared of what Zahn is awaken within me. I lessen the open space between my legs by the time he reaches his target.

"Naomi," he warns.

Not giving in, I cast my unsteady eyes on Zahn. With a frown, he overrides me with such ease, it's comical. His strong hands part my legs.

"I've waited all my life to lick you," he speaks.

"Oh gawd."

"I'm going to drown in your pussy."

"ZAHN!!"

I muffle my cries behind my shaking hand. He has to hold me down, my reaction is so violent when the tip of his masterful tongue splits my pussy lips to reach my hot, pink flesh. That's it. I'm done. I can only imagine what the people outside are hearing and saying about the noises I'm making.

Unable to contain myself, my hand falls away. Instantly, Zahn moves it to place on the top of his head. The action makes me steal a glance at him. Now, I can't look away. I watch in utter amazement while he laps at me. His tongue vanishes between my plump, shaved lips to stab my quivering hole before his mouth makes a tight seal for him to suck and hum. The vibration sends shock waves through me. Adding his fingers to the party, everything is becoming too much to handle.

Looking downward, I find his brown gaze watching me. That there is the missing piece. Remember I said the testament of a man when it comes to sex is if he can please his woman? The only way to do so is if he knows her, and only a man that really cares will strive to learn. From the beginning, that's what Zahn wanted to know...and in a matter of 30 minutes, he has shown me so much.

Only once in my life have, I experienced a spiritual moment. As a kid, I was doing a stunt on set that knock the wind out of me. I thought I saw Heaven that day. Right now, I see the face of Jesus as every nerve ending in my body explodes. My back arches off the ground, my hand tugs and grips Zahn's hair as I force him deeper into my pussy to drink while I scream his name.

See, this is why I wanted to do all of this before people got to the site. I knew this man was going to take it to me. I just didn't know that it would be to this extent. Once I gain the ability to breathe again, I'm ready for more. At the feel of Zahn positioning himself between my limp legs, he is too. I give him a crooked smirk.

"O, OOO."

"Umm, woman, your pussy is so, mmm," is his response to the friction our skin on skin is making as he penetrates me, slowly.

I said I wanted to be full, and Zahn is damn sure delivering. The sound of his moans and grunts is like music to my ears. Listening to his dirty talk as he describes how I make him feel is an empowering thing to be heard. It's nothing like knowing you have the power to bring a man, *this* man to his knees. Sliding his arm under my leg, he forces it up and back as he leans further, deeper into my body. When I think he's reached his limit, Zahn rotates his hips to show I still had room to give.

Finally satisfied, he begins to move. His strokes are slow, shallow then he switches to a faster, deeper tempo that has me holding on for dear life. The slapping sound of our bodies joins my pussy popping noises to echo throughout the tipi.

"I can't get enough, Naomi," he grunts as he opens me wider by now lifting back both of my legs.

I'm at his mercy, which is no other place I would rather be. Having experienced it twice already, I know what's building. My walls are wet with my juices, making his thrusting dick slip and slide with ease in and out. It's the deepness of his thrusts, that's beating the shit out of my insides. Even still, I'm begging him for more.

It's funny how I was cold, but now we're sporting a light sheen of sweat. My fingertips dance along his spine as I travel down to rest on his flexing ass. His fit body feels even better on top of me and fucking between my legs.

Zahn shifts his hips slightly and my pussy explodes around his throbbing dick. Now, I thought he would pause. Hell no, Zahn continues to ride my pulsating pussy hard...and thankfully so because this magic man manages to pull another orgasm out of me before he rides my ass into the sunset which is where he finds his own release.

I don't need a mirror to see my frazzled reflection. Nor do I need one to know I'm starstruck when Zahn glances down into my face. Why? Because the expression on his face is mirroring mine.

CHAPTER ELEVEN

NAOMI

"I need to get you a surgeon to remove that smile."

My smile grows into a goofy grin at Sali's comment. I roll my eyes to plant them back on Zahn's form. Even among all the other men, I can make out his dancing body. The thuds of the drums vibrate through me as I watch the opening ceremony of the Lakota's Festival. The once open site is now filled with tipis, vendors, and hundreds of people. The excitement is tangible. I can't reframe from swaying to the beat while I listen to the singing in a language that's both foreign and beautiful. I wish I knew what is being said, but not knowing doesn't take anything away from the power moment. Dressed in deerskin pants with a loincloth draped over the front and back, Zahn keeps in time. Bright, colorful feathers attached to his muscular biceps and in his hair flap in the cool breeze.

"It's time."

That's our cue. Picking up the beat, Sali and I, along with the other women standing outside of the dance circle, join the fray. To the beat, we all two-step towards the men. I hold tightly to the shawl that Zahn gave me. He looks up and smiles before making his way in my direction. As he taught me, I don't open my wrap to no other but him. Under the cloth, we dance together around the dance circle. The painting of a Red Eagle clutching its prey in his talons in flight on the back of the shawl is a visual of Zahn's Lakota spirit name.

"We're not married after this?" I tease.

"No, but it shows everyone who you belong to. Actually, we just got engaged."

I stumble over my moccasin feet.

"Symbols, Naomi...nothing more," he chuckles.

OF COURSE NOT, I think.

DON'T DO THAT, I scold myself. YOU CAN'T PUNISH HIM FOR BEING REASONABLE. I'M NOT HERE TO STAY.

I recover the beat and my beaming grin to finish the dance. Shouts ring out into the noonday sky. Things have officially kicked off.

"Give me 20 minutes," Zahn whispers, hotly in my ear.

I give him a side-eye. "Yeah, right, hours later," I huff.

"Really," he promises as he encourages me to get going with a nudge.

"Don't have me waiting, and you're roped into working," I warn.

He jerks me into his arms. I love it when he does these public displays.

"The only thing I'm working for the rest of the day is my hips," he moans.

I giggle like a schoolgirl. I feel renewed and full of energy. All I want is to be with this man. I know it's a silly notion to have when reality has to be acknowledged sooner or later. I still a glimpse of him after I walk away to make sure he's going to break away from the many people wanting his attention. He winks and nods. I like the fact that his tipi is position in the back of the field, close to the tree line path that leads back to the ranch. I frown at the sound of raised voices coming from within our tipi.

Thinking back, I see I should have slowed down. I should have lingered outside the flap to snoop, but the desire to get whomever inside out to prepare for Zahn is what drives me.

"I don't give a fuck."

I enter in time to hear Rivers snarl. I catch the response, too.

"Old bitch, this isn't about you."

My presence is felt a second later. The woman that spoke last notices me. I'm instantly on my guard. The two women with Rivers are older than Zahn and me. I'm sure neither one are ex-lovers. Then again, I could be wrong. Rivers twirls around to see me.

"Oh," she sighs. "I thought you were Zahn," she admits, down hearted.

"He's talking with the guys," I reply while walking further inside. "Something up?"

They exchange looks.

"I'm Naomi," I say since Rivers isn't making a move to introduce me.

The short, round woman speaks first.

"I'm Layla. My boy has taken a shine to your sister."

I relax a bit. "You're the terrible three's Mom," I tease.

"Ha! You know them well," she laughs.

My gaze shifting to the other woman signals for her to speak.

"Jupiter," she says, touching her chest.

"And I'm a big fat hen," hisses Rivers. "When is Zahn coming?" she insists on knowing.

"Whenever he's ready," I snip.

Rivers narrows her gaze at me.

"Tell him to come to my tipi as soon as he gets here," she orders.

I don't respond when she begins to march for the exit. The other two women cast me an apologetic smirk before falling in step. I nod at them. I notice the uneven stride of Jupiter. For a second, she seems to lose her balance as she steps and swings her other leg.

"I got it," she replies while waving off Layla.

I can only imagine what that was all about. Rivers can be sweet or ice-cold, depending on the situation. She could be like all the other people running to Zahn to fix every damn problem.

"I told you to be ready."

His deep voice pulls me back and out of my funk. I open my mouth to tell him why I'm not naked and waiting. All it takes is to witness him slowly strolling across the way to forget everything else. I crane my neck back to gaze up into his handsome face. It darkness before my eyes as a hard expression falls over his chiseled features.

"A hope you're ready for this," he speaks in a deep voice that vibrates through me.

His arm moves around me to banish the few itches remaining between us. Dropping to his needs, he gets to work. I have never tasted myself before doing so on Zahn's mouth, but the way he's eating me as I ride his face makes me wonder if I tastes that good. He seems to not be able to get enough. He won't even let me show off my dick sucking skills, much to my surprise. He takes so much pleasure in the act and it evident in his level of skill.

"Don't feel guilting, Naomi. Knowing I'm making you happy gets me off, too."

Get off, is what I do. Eating me, fingering me, then finally, fucking till my knees are sore and my pussy is raw. Man, he's good. So much so that I can't stop my mind from thinking about the other women he's given this treatment to. My thoughts have me pulling out all the stops when I force my will and take over. I want to make sure I'm not the only one missing this when it's gone. I want him to be comparing me to all the skank hoes of his past.

"Yes, Na…oh, just like that, oh baby," he groans as I deep throat his cock.

Like a farm hand, I pull on his nuts to massage them as I suck him. Popping his dick out, I spit in my hand then I proceed to give him the grapefruit treatment.

My Lord, I'm curling his toes, I acknowledge with glee.

His hands capture me by the head. Bending his knees, Zahn fucks my mouth, bucking is hips, wildly. I bring him to the point of madness. Knowing he's close, he attempts to free himself, but I keep him in my mouth. Wide eyes, his hot, white, salty cream coats the inside of my mouth. Without hesitation, I swallow with a beaming grin. Panting, Zahn plops down to stare at me dumbfounded.

ZAHN

I've fucked up, and I know it. While I lay on my side to follow the movements of Naomi's lips as she talks, I know I've created a problem. The issue isn't with her. Well, maybe that is an issue too. The fact that she doesn't seem to feel or notice the change in our relationship…yeah, that is a problem. Unlike me, where she's all I can think about. She's all I want to be around, all I want to do. The activities of the festival that used to get me going are now dull compared to spending time with her…in her, under her, beside her.

I lied earlier about the dance. It meant a lot more than symbols. It's a show of my intentions before the Tribe. The fact that I committed to being a part of the circle this year, then asking her to partner with me shows just how far down the hole I've fallen. I want someone that doesn't feel the same. I'm dreaming about a future that's never going to be.

I smile to play off the fact that I'm not even listening to her. That's okay. Just as long as she's giving me her attention and I can hear her voice, I'm fine. There's a peace being here. It's what I'll miss the most, next to making love to Naomi. I'll replay the conversations often I know once she's gone. Her level of understanding is uncanny.

Yeah, I'm gonna miss all of this, because I'm not going to make the hurt worse by hoping that it can become more. I won't ask for more, which would put a strain on the few weeks we have left.

"So," Naomi says with a loud clap. "what's the events of the night?"

I smirk as I prepare to tell her in detail how I planned on licking her till she came to get a rise out of her. Suddenly, the shouting outside gets my attention. I manage to half rise before a body falls backward through the flap, followed by Travis. My first reaction is to drag Naomi behind me to shield her from the fistfight going on.

"Hey, HEY!"

My yells go un-noticed. Travis pulls his fist back to send it crashing against the man's head, snapping it to the left. My eyes widen when I get a good look of the man's face. I take a step forward to either help Travis kick ass or to stop the fight. I don't know which one. Nor do I get a chance to choose because after seeing me, the man makes a mad dash for the exit. He collides with Travis, causing him to fall, which gives the man just enough room to escape.

"What the fuck's going on?"

Out of breath, Travis rights himself.

"The motherfucker came for Jupiter."

A scowl creases my brow. "Your sister? What did she do?" I demand to know.

Maybe Travis is too worked up to hear me because he ignores my question to ask his own.

"You were supposed to come to see Rivers. She told you, right?" he inquires, pointing to Naomi.

I glance over, accusingly at her. She works her mouth a few times before speaking.

"I, I, she was in here when I came from the dance. Then you came in, and we..." she trails off with a shrug in defense.

I'm starting to get frustrated, and it shows.

"Why was that fucker at the festival? What kinda drama did your sister bring?" I growl, getting closer to Travis.

He backs away with his hands up. "Not for me to say. You need to talk to Jup and Rivers."

Not taking kindly to his answer, I reach for him with one hand while bringing my other back to punch him in the face.

"SHE'S YOUR MOTHER!" he blurts out with a grimace.

Three words stop my fist in mid-air. Three words send my world into a tailspin. I stagger back as if I've been shot. This time, it's Travis that reaches for me to keep me on my feet. My eyes blink rapidly.

"I swear...I wanted to tell you long before now," Travis cries into my stunned face. "It wasn't my call. She was afraid to say something, to come back, but Rivers tricked her, now they know she's here an-"

I shove him out of my way as I head to leave. I'm not a slow man. In a matter of a few seconds, I connected all the dots. Abby's caught wind she's back. She must have sent Cry Wolf, a goddam sellout, to threaten Jupiter or even worse if he got a chance.

"They ran to your house," is the last thing I hear.

**

The horse is still in motion as I leap from his back. My large strides take me over the threshold into the house.

"RIVERS!" I roar.

Looking more like playing on the defensive line, Layla comes running up to block me. She pushes me back with all of her might, which isn't a lot. I quickly shove her to the side to continue onward.

"RIVERS!" I roar again.

Layla claws to get a grip on my arm. She digs her feet in, in an attempt to get me to halt.

"Please, Zahn…PLEASE," she begs. "Hold up, take a sec…for your mother, PLEASE."

I stop so abruptly that Layla crashes into me.

"Why? What's wrong? She hurt?" I rattle off.

"She flips out real easy. She's scared."

"Well, let me see-"

"What you need to do is calm your ass down, please," she adds as an afterthought.

"Okay, okay," I promise.

Hands-on my hips, I take a breath. Suddenly, I'm tired. Drained, I seek the support of a nearby wall. I pin Layla with my gaze.

"So, you knew…Wes, Graham, Gil…you all-"

"No, not my boys, not till a few days ago, but I've known. Shit, we all ran together in a gang," she admits.

"Then what happened?" I demand to know.

She glances heavenward as if asking for strength. She licks her lips while she rubs the back of her neck.

"I'll tell you because I don't know if she'll be right enough to do so," she starts. "It's really fucked up, all of it…right down to

Rivers bringing her back, knowing what would happen," she babbles, hotly. "Your dad, your BLOOD, Bradley," she pauses for a second to ensure I understand what she just confided. "well, he started messing around with Travis' little sister. Not too surprising since we all hung out together. Brad, he fell hard for Jupiter, REAL hard. We, Travis, and I warned him that his racist parents weren't going to go for that, so we told him to have fun, but don't try to make it into more than that. He had to marry Abby anyway so his old man could get her parents' land. Even after he married the white bitch, he was still in love with Jupiter. Everyone knew about the two, but we all just played stupid. That changed once word got to Abby that Bradley had a baby on her. She could kinda deal with him fuckin' around, but not the shame that he had a baby. The fact that he was comfortable enough to leave his seed, shit he was starting a whole other family. So, she sent her do boys to handle it. That's how come Jupiter left you...why she's off," she explains while tapping her temple.

I don't respond for a moment. I know the reason is that I'm preparing for her answer once I get enough strength to ask my question.

"What did they do?"

Layla shakes her head like she's trying to dislodge images from her mind.

"A setup is what it was, on a night that Abby took Bradley to a snobby event. They came to her house with guns. We looked all over for her, nothing. Travis and his dad went to the sheriff. The man didn't do shit," she spats in disgust. "She was found wandering two towns over. They messed her up," hisses Layla. "We got the med report from the doctor, but Jupiter never gave us the full details of what the men did to her...how many times, they," she trails off to swallow hard. Her voice croaks. "The doctor said he thinks they hunted her, made her run, and sicked a dog on her." She bites down on her lip to stop its trembling.

"Did he know?"

Layla knows the HE, I'm referring to.

"If Bradley knew, they all would have been dead that day," she replies, fiercely. "Which is why we never told. Jupiter was screwed up in her head, too gone to raise you. Bradley came back to find she was gone, and we lied to him to make him believe she just up and went. We fought him over bringing you to this hell hole. Deep down, he knew Abby did something, and him raising you, here was everyday proof of his love for Jupiter. Why he made you believe you were adopted?" she shrugs. "I don't know, but if I had to guess, was to shut Abby the hell up about you living here."

I need a drink. I say nothing as I shuffle off for the kitchen. The first two drinks of whiskey are to stop the ringing in my ears. The next two are to control my racing heartbeat. The next one is for clarity to help with how I'm going to plot my revenge. I taste the liquor on my lips as I head in the direction Layla told me Rivers and Jupi- my mother is held up in.

"She's in his private office," Rivers announces when I poke my head into the room.

My eyebrow notches upward.

"She's been here before?"

Rivers gives me a beaming smile as she peers into the past. "Many, many times, when they wouldn't get caught. That room, she decorated," she confides.

Down the hall, around the corner, down a few steps, I finally enter into the only room in the house where I was the only one full display. All my honor roll certificates, every reward, and ribbon, my face centered in every picture frame, were kept in this room. Now, it made sense why. It was more going on than Bradley doing it to piss off Abby and send a fuck you to his other kids. It was because Jupiter wanted it that way.

In spite of me entering the room on silent footsteps, she feels my presence without looking away from the picture frame in her hand. Her back is to me. I take her in from the tip of her bent head to her socked feet. She's nothing like I imagined. Her raven's colored hair is cut to stop at the end of her neck. Her shoulders are straight. Her body is lean and firm. Small hips, I take note, which is nothing like the women in Travis' family. She's tall, too. That means only her, Graham, and Gil to have broken with that norm, also. It's when she sways, slightly on her feet that I narrow my gaze to notice the difference in her legs.

"I took this picture."

Jupiter breaks the silence. I watch the way her hand gently caresses the happy image of Bradley.

"He said that was his favorite place in the world."

"Did he?" she chuckles. "He picked up our habit of speaking with deeper meaning. He was such a ham."

She didn't need to turn for me to see the sad smile on her face. I could hear it in her voice. She slowly places the frame back down, then moves to one of mine hanging on the wall.

"You were so cute," she gushes. "Not, to say you aren't handsome," she adds in a rush while taking a glimpse of me over her shoulder. "But all these chunky rolls are gone," she coos.

"Thankfully," I huff.

"What's happening here?" she inquires.

There's a tension in the room along with a big, fat elephant that we're both trying to handle. I go to Jupiter's side. She's so tiny compared to me.

"Oh," I chuckle. "Field day in…3rd, maybe 4th, I can't remember. I didn't win any of the contests. I swore up and down that the coach was cheating me. Must have been right about it cause Bradley left and came back with that trophy," I nod towards the gold plated thing on the shelf.

"You didn't call him, Dad?"

I can feel her eyes on me. I take a steady breath and cast my eyes upon her. My heart flutters. In my dreams is the only place I thought to see my mother. Now, to have her in the flesh, gazing up at me is wreaking havoc on me. I thought I was over not having her in my life. Yet, my emotions are proving to me otherwise.

"I stopped in my teens," I admit.

"Why?"

I drop my eyes to the floor. There's no heat in her voice to make me feel shame, but I do.

"I, I felt like he wasn't my father, so I stopped. I let the things that went on in the house bother me to the point that it affected our relationship. I wish I never stopped," I finish in a whisper.

Her soft hand cups my face.

"Silly boy, it takes more than a name to tarnish the love of father and son."

I raise my own misty eyes to lock on to her red-rimmed ones.

"I hope you're right," I sigh.

"I know I am because Bradley couldn't get enough of you. Always talking about you, praising you, you, you," chimes Jupiter. "If you weren't mine, I might have had a case of envy."

The revelation causes me to stiffen. Not only didn't I hear all that praise, but I didn't know she and Bradley had reconnected. If that's the case, why the hell he didn't tell me the truth? Why the fuck didn't she come back? The energy in the room changes instantly. I step back as if her touch burned me. It takes everything within me not to be led by the conflicting thoughts competing in my brain.

"Let me explain," she offers. There's a hint of fear in her tone.

"Well, yes, please," I reply firmly.

"I left when-"

"You don't have to relive that with me. If I hear more about it, I'll snap," I growl. "Your leg...from that too?"

Her nod is all the answer she gives. Reaching down, I lift the hem of her dress. I don't blink or look away from the ugly scar, and the missing muscle and flesh from the dog bite. I want all the information to ensure when I go calling for payback, I'll exact the full price owed to me and mine.

"How, when did you and Brad-dad start seeing each other again?" I ask.

"We only had a few years before he died. He never stopped wondering, searching. It seems the older I got, I stop caring about dying. I just wanted to see him again, be with him...if he still wanted me," Jupiter shrugs. "I showed up at one of the cattle sells. Lord, that man," she laughs. "He about caused a stampede when he caught sight of me across the arena. I mean, he ran, made a beeline THROUGH the showing circle, spooking the herds, and damn near got trampled just to reach me," she recounts with pride and love. "I told him to be content. I didn't need to be with him every day. I was happy with us being together, whenever...but you know your daddy," she groans.

"He was going to leave it all," I remark in disbelief. "That's why he turned everything over to me, had me running the ranch and business," I go on in awe. Suddenly, something else hit me.

"The people that hurt you did you ever tell him who they were?" I press.

Jupiter's eyes shift, but not before I read the truth in their depths. The long game. It's a trait that my father taught me well. So, all the motherfuckers giving me grief over my land can all thank Bradley for their inheritance. Thanks to him, their time of waiting for their fathers to kick the bucket was sped up by many years. One by one, spaced out over a matter of three years, I bet he was the reason for all of those men's deaths.

"All he had to do was be content," she repeats, sadly. "You can't do the things he did and not think to have to pay one day. Even if I was wrong about how he died, I wasn't going to take a chance when it came to you, Zahn. You're all I have left of him."

Bullshit. Brad's death had nothing to do with paying for putting those cold bastards down. Nah, his death hinged on the fact he was finally going to live the life stolen from him. Even after all the years she had taken from him, Abby still couldn't deal with seeing him happy in the arms of another. No one can make me believe that she didn't kill my father.

CHAPTER TWELVE

NAOMI

I feel like shit right about now. No matter what I do, I can't shake the fact that I messed up. The way Zahn looked at me turned my blood cold. Then to find out the woman is his damn mama!

"Damn it!" I exclaim.

I lost count of the times I've paced around the tipi. As the hours tick by, I sink further into worry. Should I leave? If Zahn is upset because I didn't send him over to Rivers, I don't want to be here for it. I don't want to admit to him it was my selfishness that caused…caused what? Did someone come to ruff the poor woman up to scare her back into her cave?

"Lord," I cry as I place my palm to my forehead.

These people are crazy, no dangerous. From Rivers talking about making people disappear to Zahn confessing to murder, I'm fucking around with danger. I test the weight of my cell as I stare at my reflection in the screen. My head snaps up at the rustling sound of the flap. My eyes widen in my eagerness to gauge Zahn's mood.

"I'm not drunk," he promises with a wave of a bottle in his hand. "I just need a drink, a few drinks," he corrects. "Who were you talking to?" he questions while eying my phone.

"Nobody," I answer.

Tossing it on a nearby pillow I stop myself from badgering him with a million questions.

"I'm so, so SO sorry for forgetting to tell you what Rivers said," I breathe.

"Forget, or you had other things pressing?" he smirks.

His sly smile gives me hope.

"I didn't forget. I, I was being selfish with your time. People are always calling for you...and I wanted you...for me," I admit.

His gaze doesn't leave mine while he takes a sip from his full glass of what I'm guessing is whiskey.

"Please tell me she's okay, though. Whoever that guy was didn't get to her?" I ask with my hand on my chest.

"She's okay."

I didn't even realize I was holding my breath until it came out in a loud exhale. I close my eyes as I send up praise.

"My father killed them all, but I'm going to do a lot more than that."

Zahn's tone is even, sane...too sane. Maybe that's why what he said is so chilling. His brown eyes are narrow slits. He's calculating, forming a plan in such a calm way. I can't move from under the intensity of his stare.

"History repeating itself," he says, mindlessly. "Every motherfucker that's been fighting me tooth and nail...well, the sins of their fathers will be like an undertow drowning each and every one," his eyes shifts as if they are finally focusing on me. "It will take a moment for the chemicals I have poisoning their land to take effect. Little by little, the yield will be less and less to the point that NOTHING will grow in the soil. The dead seeds they sold me years ago, I've found a way to sell it back to them. Boom, no crops," he smiles, wickedly as he tilts his head. "In about a month or less, the bank is going to come calling to collect on the millions of dollars they've borrowed over the years. How that's going to turn out when crops they have been able to grow become tainted on the vine...the cattle are dying in the field because of the poisoned irrigation. All these things I've put into motion. Now the outcome will be even more sweeter when they lose every...fucking...thing."

Zahn raises his glass in salute before doing it in one swallow. I don't know what to say. What I do know is I'm at least happy not to have just heard him share his plot of committing and getting away with murder. The things he did tell me are stuff that white farmers have been playing at against blacks for years to gain our land or push us out of the agriculture industry — nothing new to see here. I'm at odds of what should happen next.

"I can bunk with Sali if you want to bring-"

"No," he sighs while getting to his feet. "You can stay. I have to go take care of her."

"Oh," I reply.

ARE YOU COMING BACK? Is the question burning on the top of my tongue? The thought of me saying it has SELFISH written all over it. Zahn finally has his mother. He could claim all he wants about getting over the fact he never had her growing up. All that shit went out the window once they were reunited. They have years to catch up on, words that need to be spoken, a bond that is necessary to be mended.

I awkwardly move around the tipi as he changes into jeans and a t-shirt.

"Be safe."

He pauses at the flap. Call me what you want. Seeing him getting ready to leave without saying goodbye kinda hurt. I wish I knew what he's thinking when he glances back at me. A weak grin is all he gives me before he disappears.

"Shit," I hiss.

For the next five hours, I mull around the festival. I don't want to bring Sali's down with my drama. I watch the horse races, stuff my face with way too much fatty food, and talk to whomever willing to converse. With a corn dog in my hand, I lean over the railing to await the next festival event.

"When are you going to fix your face?"

My body stiffens as it instantly reacts to his deep voice. Zahn's strong arms maneuvers around me before I can turn. Resting his chin on the top of my head, he pulls me tight against him. I marvel at how my mood changes with his presence. I didn't want to acknowledge it before, but I want this man.

"The sun's in my eyes," I lie.

"Really? Even in the shade?" he teases. "Ouch!" he cries at my elbow to the ribs.

"Are you just checking in before leaving?"

I pray my tone is normal. I pray it isn't too much hope there...or annoyance from missing him.

"There's nothing I can do about the past, but I have power over the present. I want you, Naomi. I don't want to miss a second with you," he whispers hotly in my ear. "We die once, but I can choose how I live...love," he adds, slowly.

Love? That term holds so many meanings. It could mean his bulge pressing into my ass or the rhythm of my heart. Confusing the two can lead to unspeakable pain. We watch the activities for another hour before walking, hands entwined, back to our tipi.

CHAPTER THIRTEEN

ZAHN

I let my mind wander while I wait for the bitch to arrive. I welcome the time. I toss one leg over the other and relax. At long last, the time to put an end to this shit has come. For two days, I juggled spending time with Jupiter, moving the chess pieces across the board, but most of my days were with Naomi.

"Hum," I moan as I snuggle deeper into the leather seat.

Naomi. Just the thought of her, saying her name brings a smirk to my face. I have no fucking idea what she and I are doing. All I know is I like it. Every day, I mentally tick off another day spent as I count down to the end of her stay. Tomorrow will bring it to a little more over a week left.

I listen to the sound of doors closing. A set of keys clink into the hand glass bowl in the foyer. Footsteps echo, bringing her closer to the atrium in at the foot of the grand staircase. The sight of me drains the bit of color from her spray-tanned face. True to form, Abby recovers quickly.

"How did you get in here?"

I ignore her question.

"I preferred to come see you before you ordered another assassination attempt."

She has enough sense to play dumb.

"Are you talking about that bitch, Jupiter?" she chuckles. "Why the hell would I worry about her?" she huffs.

I won't take the bait.

"The fact that you're aware that she's even here is omission enough," I smirk. "I'm here to make you an offer," I say. I'm ready for the smell of blood.

"Not Jonelle's grand plan to marry you. That damn girl is out of her ever-loving mind. I'm leaving you with not one red penny... pun intended," she chuckles at her tasteless joke.

"No cunt. I'm giving you the chance to hobble your wrinkle ass into the shadows."

"Fuck you," she hisses. "Get the fuck out," she spits.

Getting to my feet, I nod. "It's no sweat off my sack. You can be the biggest joke once I make it know that Bradley is my Dad, my blood."

For an older woman, Abby can move. She dots in front of me to halt me from leaving.

"Fuckin', liar!" she yells.

"That's not what my birth certificate says."

"There was no certificate. She had you at home."

I keep my expression void of the anger I'm fighting to remain below the surface.

"You are an idiot. The place of my birth doesn't make a difference. I'm on paper."

Abby searches my face as she considers my statement. Now, for the nail.

"Then there's the other nurse that helped at my birth. It seems Rivers wasn't the only one. There's nothing like a white woman's testimony to make everything true," I beam.

"Who?" she questions, narrowing her gaze.

"By this time tomorrow, you and everyone in the state will know," I promise.

Done, I stroll by Abby towards the door. I know I won't make it before she calls out to me.

"Wait! Wait!"

I take another wide step just to make the bitch run after me.

"Give me the earnings from the cattle drive," she offers.

Millions...with an S is what she's demanding. I stare at her as if she's stuck on stupid.

"You must not understand the concept of, THE UPPER HAND."

"I'll fight it in court. I swear! I'll drag that prairie niggar bitch, destroy her family," threatens Abby.

"You can't fight DNA."

I can't stop the crazy laugh that explodes from my twisted lips.

"I'll make sure the press is there, too, when the old man's dug up. I think that would be a perfect time to have Jupiter tell her story at the gravesite. With him above ground, I can test my theory of how he really died," I slow down on that last sentence as I pin Abby with my hard gaze.

I'm witnessing the cracking in her armour.

"Who's gonna sign off on that?"

"Money isn't the only cuckold. I have shit on certain people far, FAR worse. I have shit to do. I'll leave you to your doubts."

Her bony hand bites into my arm to make me stay. I hide my clenched fist. She killed my father. The stark fear widening her pale blue eyes says it all.

"Fine," she hisses.

"I'm no fool to believe lips service with no proof. I want you to call Coby, tell him it's all off," I demand.

Abby cranes her head back to look me over.

"Why worry about him? He's just a toothless dog on a leash."

"And you can say whatever in private and change up tomorrow. I want to HEAR you tell your boy you're dropping out," I order with a nudge towards the sitting room's phone.

Abby stumbles back, then gains her footing. She's eyeing me closely. Her head turns towards the open dark archway of the room, then back over to me.

"No," she snaps. "I'll call from here," she announces as she digs out her cell from the purse clutched in her hand.

I roll my eyes. "In a house with a mouse, on a train in the rain, I don't give a fuck...and put it on speaker, so I know it's really him you called."

Leaning on the wall, I listen to every angry word. I try to let the slanderous shit said about me, the threats made against everyone I love, and my Tribe wash over me. Coby is a cold motherfucker, just like his old man. Now, I wish I had cum in his wife and fucked his daughters when they asked to share my dick.

"Done, now get the fuck out," she growls while she stabs the button on her cell to end the call. "You think you won?" she scoffs. "Give me some time. I'm going to fuck you over, I swear," she says, hatefully.

I narrow my eyes.

"Loose ends usually do...which is why I don't leave any."

A slow, wicked smirk spreads across my lips. Removing my shoulder from the wall, I nod my head. Confused, Abby spins around just in time to see the forms emerge from the dark sitting room. When she turns back in my direction, her confused expression is replaced with fear.

"Have fun, ladies," I chuckle.

"Oh, we will...won't we, Abby," replies Rivers.

Layla, Travis's aging mother, and Jupiter come to stand next to Rivers. I meet Wes and Gil at the front door.

"Don't let them drag it out too long," I warn.

"Here," remarks Gil while handing me over the recording of the Abby and Coby's phone call. I pass to him the small listening device I had set up in the house.

"Dump her in Coby's hog pen. There should be enough of her left for the police to find in a few days," is the last statement I make.

Forty-eight hours, on the last day of the festival, the cops come with gun blazing with Coby leading the charge. I listen to the man calmly as he lays out the case against me. When asked if all Coby says is true, I don't lie. Instead, I take great pleasure in blowing his case to hell.

"What fuck boy doesn't know is that I don't need to jump through hoops because the land is mine, outright."

"Bullshit! We got the law on our side. You knew it. That's why you did something to Abby," accuses Coby.

"Abby?" I repeat as I tilt my head. "Sounds real friendly. I guess it didn't come up in the afterglow that the old bitch didn't have a case because I'm Bradley's son," I hold my hand up to shut the asshole up. "Not on paper, but BLOOD...as in he was fucking around on Abby for years. Somebody give this boy a glass of water before he faints," I tease.

The chief of police lowers his eyes. He's old enough to have heard the rumors.

"Why you think I didn't care whenever she rode on her broom to cause me drama. Shit, I just let her talk," pausing, I pretend to be surprised. "You actually fell...you let her con you out of dick," tossing back my head, I laugh.

"Mr. Ewring," the chief cautions.

"I'm sorry," I cough. "You're right. The woman is missing," I nod. My gaze falls on Coby. "Well, what happened after she called you to tell you she was dropping the suit? Any hints of where she could be?"

I let the words fall from my lips, nonchalantly. All eyes become glued on Coby.

"Call?" presses the chief.

"Abby plays the same game every few months. She'll come in like a storm, demanding money. I give her the cash, and she takes her ass down the road. I didn't think anything different this time. I have a recording of her talking to Coby, telling him that she was dropping the case. He cussed her out, talking about being in debt and needing his share to keep things running...well, shit, you tell'em," I order, giving Coby the floor.

A deer caught in headlights. Each face Coby turned to for understanding, mercy, all he found was accusations. A head gesture from the chief signals to the policemen flanking Coby to move closer. There's no place the man can run, but that might not stop him from trying to get lost in the sea of people or the woods.

"I'm sorry for bothering you, Mr. Erwing."

"No, bother. I'll get the recording over to you," I promise.

"Um, don't want to step on any toes, but it's only been rumors about your father. I'll need to see the proof," explains the chief.

I smile. Of course, you won't take the word of an Indian.

"I'll bring it. If that isn't good enough, you can ask to talk to Mrs. Collins. She was the second midwife at the birth. Her memory isn't shot. Then there's Judge Murphy. He was an eyewitness to what my Dad was doing. He has nothing to lose by telling the truth."

"Thank you, Sir," replies the chief with a tip of his ten-gallon cowboy hat.

Yeah, the sooner Judge Murphy does his part, the sooner I can tip his name with all the info I have on him to the FEDS. If he thinks I'm going to let him continue to rape little black kids, he has scrambled eggs for brains.

"Nicely done," says Naomi, coming up behind me. "Very believable, not too forced, natural."

I cut my eyes at her. I don't respond. Somethings are better left unsaid.

"Can we enjoy the rest of our time?"

THE REST OF OUR TIME. Seven days left...or so I thought.

—

CHAPTER THIRTEEN

I blink as I read the text for the second time. I made sure to rise earlier than usual to ensure I got all my work with the animals done to give Naomi and me a free day. I should know never to plan. If you don't live with expectations, it doesn't hurt when they don't come true.

HEADS UP. INVESTORS ARE DEMANDING A QUICK START. WANT TO MAKE SURE SHE'S WORTH THE MONEY BEFORE GOING ALL IN, I GUESS. TEST FILMING STARTS ASAP. SORRY.

I strangle my phone. It's not going to erase Austin's message. Nor does it help to calm me. The seven days we had left is now being cut short by three. Three days of hoping that something would happen or change to make Naomi stay. Three more days of dancing around the coming break. Three more days of me wanting to ask for more, fighting the temptation of begging her to stay, me going out of my way to show her how much I care.

I have to force one foot in front of the other. Anger is what I feel when I round the house to find a hired car already waiting to take Naomi and Sali away. She sure is getting shit in order in a hurry, huh? Already, she's forgetting me, ready to move on.

ISN'T THAT WHAT WAS GOING TO HAPPEN ANYWAY? NOW OR THREE DAYS FROM NOW, SHE WAS GOING TO LEAVE.

Fuck rational thinking. I know I'm the fool for falling for this woman. Didn't I warn Graham not to do the same thing? How many times have I told the women I fucked not to get attached? Yet here I am...with my heart on my sleeve as I stand in the doorway of my room, watching Naomi pack. She's mumbling to herself. A habit I've come to enjoy.

"Making sure you have everything?"

I stroll in, casting my gaze around the room to hold off from looking at her.

I NEED MORE TIME, I cry, mentally, but I won't say it. I refuse to play the fool. I won't make this harder on myself than it already is.

"Excited?" I go on, instead.

Naomi gives me a weak smile.

"A little...more nervous than anything," she admits while rubbing her palms on her pants. "I know I have to wow them."

"Well, I can testify to your riding skills," I tease.

The sound of her laughter isn't as free coming as I remember it to be. Naomi shifts her weight.

"I'm sorry to be leaving like this."

"I understand," I nod.

Lord the awkwardness, the tension is stifling.

"Why are we acting this way? It's not like we can't see each other if we wanted to."

She wants to know where we stand. I see it now. I'm not the only one that was hoping. It's wishful thinking, though. Or maybe it's to make going our separate ways an easier pill to swallow.

"We're both old enough to know. I'll only speak on myself when I say, I'm here. I made sure to show you that I'm here. I chose you when the shit hit the fan."

"I'm not casting you aside, Zahn. I shouldn't have to choose."

"Then don't...and don't make promises you can't keep."

There's no heat in my tone. I even grin and give her a wink before I quit the room, the house, and the entire goddamn county. I need space.

NAOMI

Funny how much I've come to relay of Zahn to keep me stable. As I sit on the plane, waiting to fly away, I feel a hint of slight fluttering of my heart. It's the same old sensations of a mild panic attack. My desire to prove that I won't be the same person I was when I came here, I still by hand from fishing in my purse for my pills. Instead, I concentrate on my breathing while chanting the song I learned at the festival. I don't know the entire meaning of all the words Zahn taught me to sing in Lakota. It's just the fact that it brings back a moment we shared that helps to still my mounting fears.

"Finally, I thought I was going to have to leav..." my words trail off at the sight of the person entering the plane after Sali.

My heartbeat accelerates. The butterflies in my stomach take off as my mind begins to race with possibilities. Quickly, Sali leans over to whisper.

"Zahn isn't coming, *just* Graham."

My eyes lock with Graham. He knows what she's telling me as he strolls further into the plane to find a seat.

"Okay," I mumble with a nod.

EPILOGUE

ZAHN

To say I'm goddamn tired is an understatement. For months I've overworked myself to ensure when my head hit the pillow, I would be out like a light. It was the only thing that helped. That shit had to stop, though, before I worked myself into an early grave. It wasn't a complete cure, but it took the edge off, at least. I didn't want to, but I was the first one to break and call. Hearing her voice soothed and caused me pain. Even still, we kept up the back and forth until it happened. I would call, and she was too busy. Finally, I just stopped altogether.

The loss hit me harder than I thought it would. Who the fuck said it's better to have loved than not at all are fucking morons. It's better not to have experienced what you're missing, is how it should go. Knowing what I've lost has taken the life out of me. What used to bring me at least joy is like a chore nowadays. I feel aged. Worse, I feel like a goddamn fool for thinking that she would stay… or make an attempt. Then again, I was the one that told her not to make any promises.

The familiar smell hits my nose when I enter the kitchen.

"Chili," I frown as I walk over to the pot.

I told Rivers not to make this shit, and not just because she makes it so bland. It reminds me of Naomi. If that's the case, I need to pack up and move out because ever where I look or go reminds me of that damn woman.

Gripping the side handles of the pot, I jerk it from the hot stove eye. I back up to head for the garbage only to freeze. Dazed and confused, I glare at the can of mixed seasoning shoved into my face. No, it's more than that.

WHEN DID RIVERS' HAND GET SO DARK? I wonder, stupidly.

Slowly, my gaze roams up the hand to the arm. By the time my eyes reach the head, they are as wide as the giddy grin on my face. The pot falls hard back to the stove. In awe, I take in the most beautiful sight. No longer in my dreams, I breathe in her smell.

Without a word, Naomi places the seasoning on the countertop. I remain rooted in place as she approaches. Suddenly, Naomi stops to stare into my stunned face. Palms flat on my chest, I know she has to feel the racing of my heart.

"I missed you so much."

I'm ready to show her how much I've missed her, but she pulls back her head before I can capture her lips.

"Zahn, Zahn wait," she says in a rush. "Remember when I asked if you could make it last? You said it was up to me, that it's my choice," she pauses to press her point home. "I want this, us. You were right." She forces my head down by pulling on my neck as she rolls up on the tips of her toes. "We only die once, so I need to choose how I spend my every day," she breathes into my parted mouth.

MY WOMAN, is all I can think as I ingest Naomi's kiss of life.

"You know, we're too old for all the drama. I think we need to cut the shit and just get married," I suggest. "It will take all the guesswork out of things."

"Wow, what a proposal," she scoffs. "No bended knee."

"Well, my knees pop. What if I can't get back up?" I tease.

"That's a damn lie," she chuckles.

Getting serious, I drop to one knee with ease while drawing her close. Naomi grips my face between her hands.

"I wanna make it last," she moans into my face.

"And it shall... till our dying days."

THE END

Hello Peeps!

I have to say, I really enjoyed writing about an older, seasoned couple. It's something about two people that have been there, done that, and now are wise enough to know what they want when they see it. Needless to say, Zahn and Naomi really deserved their HEA.

Now, on to Austin and Dani! Oh, the drama and laughs dealing with those two. Can't wait for you guys to read it. Until then…thanx so much for the support, the reviews, and the shares. I'm here only because of each and every one of you.

Much Luv,

Christine Gray.

FACEBOOK:

https://www.facebook.com/SapphirelRRomanceFanPg/

INSTAGRAM:

https://www.instagram.com/christinegraysapphire/

PERSONAL WEBSITE:

https://www.christinesappgrayauthor.com/

MY BOOKS READING ORDER
**To dates, I have over 35 books published. If you are stuck on the order of which to read, here's a list.
Starting with my pen name <u>SAPPHIRE</u>**

The Order:

Don't Tell My Husband Series
Falling For an Alpha Billionaire
Consumed By Love
Extraordinary Love; Angie and Levi's Story
One Of A Kind Love Series

THEN, next are CHRISTINE GRAY:

The Billionaire Mob Wife
Pursued; A Billionaire Obsession
Sweet Obsession; Her Beast, His Beauty
Dirty; Loving Him Against The Odds
No One Can Love You Like I Can Series
Irish Heat; Claiming His Heart
Relentless; A Vampire King's Desire Series
Fated To Love
Fated To Be Mine
Fated To Bleed
Fated Till The End
Unchain My Heart; Edwin and Jenalle Romance
Tainted Love
Forbidden Lust
Don't Walk Away; Elmo and Christine Romance
Blindsighted By Love; Cujo and Rhi's Romance
Enjoying Mr. Hardwood Series
Case File:01- The Pervert, The Monster, and The Sex-Bot
Case File:02- The Savage, The Pretenders, and The Hunch, Punch Train
Case File:03- The Fool, The Scrooge, and The Slutty Elf On The Shelf
Case File:04- The Damned, The Jackal, And The Cocopuff Pimp

Book 5- The Twisted King, The Naive Lover, and The House OF Joy And Pain
A Desert King's Obsession Series
I'll Be Good To You
Case File:06- The Disgruntle Pumpkins, The Five Live Crew, and The Halloween Of Whores Patch
Just Say Yes

Looking for a publishing home?

After Hours Publications, is accepting submissions from motivated, talented Authors Experienced and NON- Experienced with a knack of creating drama filled, romantic, downright sappy stories desired. SHORT STORIES with a min of 18k words, also welcomed.

If you are a lover of Interracial Romance, AHP is the publishing house for you; Contemporary, Paranormal, Historical, New Adult Romance. Interested? Submit the first 3-4 chapters with your synopsis to Submissions@afterhourspublications.com.

Check out our website for more information:

www.afterhourspublications.com

Be sure to LIKE our After Hours Publications page on Facebook.

MAKE IT LAST

CPSIA information can be obtained
at www.ICGtesting.com
Printed in the USA
LVHW041658061120
670968LV00006B/996